COLD DARK HEART

JULIE KRISS

ONE

Damon

I DIDN'T SEE the kid at first. He was standing behind a rack of magazines, and he was turned toward the glass door of the soda fridge, as if the bottles of Dr. Pepper were fascinating. I had to give him credit: until I saw the top of his head in the fisheye mirror in the corner above the gas station clerk, I had no idea he was there.

I usually had better instincts than that. Then again, my instincts weren't what they used to be.

"Thirteen bucks," the woman behind the counter said. She was sixtyish, her gray hair scraped back into a ponytail that looked painful, her polyester shirt hanging loosely on her bony frame.

I rifled through my wallet, glancing at the kid in the mirror reflection again. He hadn't moved. "Add a pack of smokes," I said, taking out another bill.

The lady slapped the pack onto the counter. "You should quit," she said. "I got lung cancer twice. It's a sonofabitch."

"Yeah?" I said, pushing the money across the counter. She had the raspy voice of a longtime smoker. "Did you quit?"

She made a disgusted sound and took my money.

"I didn't think so." I looked at the reflection of the kid again. How old was he? Thirteen, fourteen? What fourteen-year-old kid hung out in a gas station in the middle of Wherever the Fuck, Colorado?

Then I saw why. While the lady was busy with my change, the kid silently opened the soda fridge and slid a bottle into his jacket. Then, just as deftly, he did the same thing with a bag of chips. He sidled along the aisle toward the door.

Oh, hell. This was just what I needed. Now I could either be an accessory to a petty shoplifting crime, or I could be the asshole who snitches on a kid.

This should be an easy question. I had just spent eight years as a cop—though a federal one. Shoplifting hadn't been my area of expertise. If the kid had been carrying cocaine or meth, I would know exactly what to do. As it was, I watched in the mirror as he walked out the door with his illicit snack, the digital bell pinging as the door closed behind him.

I pulled an extra five from my wallet and gave it to the lady behind the counter. "Take this."

She frowned. "What's this for?"

"To pay for the chips and drink that kid just stole from your store."

I thought it was a pretty good compromise. The store gets paid, the kid doesn't get hurt. Everybody wins except my wallet.

I was wrong. The woman snatched my five, but she also flew into action. "That little shit. I've seen him in here before." She came out from behind the counter and sprinted for the door, making the digital bell go off again. "You little fucker!" she shouted, surprisingly loud for a woman with bad lungs. "See how you like that bottle when it's shoved up your ass!"

I could see the kid sprinting through the parking lot toward a waiting car, probably driven by one of his friends. The woman sprinted after him, still shouting. The kid sped up in terror and jumped into the car, which sped away.

I let the door shut behind me as I watched the scene. As the woman caught her breath and turned to come back, I pulled one of the cigarettes from the pack and lit it.

"Nice try," I said as she approached. "You got close."

"Thanks for the help, asshole," she barked.

I shrugged. My days fighting the bad guys—even when the bad guys were kids—were over. "Want one?" I held the pack out to her.

She looked at the cigarettes, then glared at me. She wanted one, all right. Badly. "Go fuck yourself," she said.

"You sure? They're delicious."

"Fuck off and die." She walked past me and went into the store. She had a pretty good swearing vocabulary for an older lady. Maybe she had grandkids to teach her.

I stood in front of the gas station, smoking my cigarette and wondering for the hundredth time if I should turn around and go back. The question was, go back where? I had no home to go, no place that called to me. In my years in the DEA, I'd moved from place to place—Florida, New Mexico, California for a while. None of them were supposed to be home, so I hadn't treated them like home. They were places to stay while I completed an investigation, and when the investigation was over, I'd move on to the next one.

Until I'd been shot twice, and I wasn't going to do any investigations again.

The only direction to go now was forward, to the job that

was waiting for me in this place I'd never been to before. The air was crisp with spring and the breeze tossed clouds past the mountains in the distance. I was alone in this parking lot, with nothing but myself and silence.

"Welcome to Colorado," I said out loud.

Then I dropped my cigarette, ground it out, and went back to my car.

THE RADIO DIAL was packed with country music, because of course it was. This was the cowboy part of the country, at least according to Hollywood. What it would be like in real life, I had no idea.

I was driving through the town of Salt Springs, just outside of Denver. It was a good-sized town, with local art galleries and stores selling handmade crafts. I saw young people hanging around, and I remembered from my Google searches that there was a community college nearby. It seemed lively on a sunny spring day. What puzzled me was why Terry, my old acquaintance, had said that he ran a bar here. A bar apparently big enough to need a guy like me to head up security. I'd immediately pictured a strip club or a multi-level nightclub in a dank downtown somewhere, not this clean-cut place. What kind of bar had Terry been talking about?

Too late, it occurred to me that I could have done a little more research—or any research at all—before getting in my car and accepting Terry's invitation to give me a job, sight unseen. I'd done it because I was at loose ends. My career with the DEA was over. My health was shot to shit, which was the reason for the career thing. I didn't have a wife or kids or any of the other things a lot of guys have by age thirty-seven. Working undercover for years tends to guarantee you don't make connections.

So, with that part of my life over, I'd had no idea what to do. Until Terry sent me an email, saying he'd heard through the DEA grapevine that I was free now, and he needed someone like me. Someone he trusted to take care of his bar here in Salt Springs, Colorado. He needed me to start right away, and was I interested?

It wasn't as weird a request as it seemed. Retired agents could get pretty sweet gigs through the grapevine like this—we had skills, after all, and we knew how to use them. Some guys got jobs doing high-level secret security for corporations, or doing personal bodyguard work for rich people or celebrities. Terry had been an agent like me, though I had only worked with him once or twice. I remembered he'd left to take a job doing a private security contract for, I assumed, very good money. He must have used that good money to buy a bar.

And that, right there, was the sum of my information. I had no idea why Terry had bought—or possibly started—a bar business. I had no idea why a qualified security guy couldn't be found in Colorado. I'd only known that I needed a job and a destination to head to, and Terry had offered me both. Frankly, I'd just wanted to get the hell out of Texas.

I had nothing against Texas, except for the fact that my brother and his soon-to-be wife, who was also his ex-wife, were there. And *that* situation was one I wanted to get away from.

My GPS told me that I had arrived at my destination, saving me from thinking too much about Texas.

The place was definitely a bar. It was two stories, the front styled like an old-time saloon. The cheesiness would be hard to fathom if it wasn't right there in front of my eyes. Neon letters, not yet lit, hung across the building's front, forming the words: THE WILD WILD WEST.

I drove around the side of the building and parked in the small lot at the back. I turned my car off and took a breath, running a hand through my hair. I had the sudden feeling that Terry wasn't serious about his offer, that maybe he'd been pranking me. Though it would be a pretty fucking cruel prank.

There was only one way to find out. I was here now, and I had nowhere else to go, at least for tonight. The only thing for it was to go inside and face whatever was next.

I got out of the car and circled back to the front of the building. It was four in the afternoon, and the bar was open. I opened the wooden door and stepped inside.

It was dark in here, and my eyes had to adjust. It was a big place, with a huge first-floor room and an open staircase to a second level. Along one wall was a bar made to look like something from a Western, and there was a raised stage in the back corner which presumably was for a band. At this time of day there were only a few people in here, the daytime regulars and alcoholics who never missed a day. The atmosphere was tired and sleepy.

Working behind the bar was a guy of about sixty who would have scored highly in a Kenny Rogers lookalike contest. "Help you?" he asked me.

"Hey," I said, approaching the bar. "I'm looking for Terry."

Kenny Rogers frowned at me. "Terry ain't here."

"Is he around somewhere? He's expecting me."

Kenny frowned harder, like he'd smelled something bad. "You a friend of his?"

"More of a business acquaintance."

"You a Fed?"

"I was," I said. "What's with the questions?"

Kenny wiped his hands on a towel. "What's your name, son?"

"Damon Blake."

"I'll ask the boss." He turned and went into the back room without another word.

I didn't have long to wait. A few minutes later, Kenny came back out. Behind him was a woman.

A gorgeous woman.

She had dark hair in long curls, tied in a messy ponytail on top of her head. She was wearing an olive green tank top that showed off sleek shoulders and elegant, toned arms. When she came out from behind the bar, I could see that she was wearing jeans that fit her like a dream and ankle boots. She was fucking stunning. The problem was, she was scowling at me.

"Who are you?" the woman asked me. "What do you want?"

"Who are you?" I asked back.

"You're in my bar, so you better answer first."

Her bar? I thought this was Terry's bar. "I'm an old colleague of Terry Brewster's," I said. "My name is Damon. He told me he needed to hire a head of security. He told me to show up and start right away."

The hot woman still scowled at me. Behind the bar, Kenny Rogers was still scowling, too. The air was practically frigid. I had the feeling that I had somehow made a very big mistake.

"Well, I'm sorry you wasted your time, but you can get lost," the woman said. "I'm Terry's wife—soon to be his ex-wife. If you want to talk to Terry, you'll have to get his new number or find him in Florida. Terry left town with his girlfriend two weeks ago. This bar is mine now. And you can go home."

TWO

Andie

THE MAN in my bar didn't move. He just stood there, surprise flickering behind his gray eyes.

"He left?" he asked.

"Sure he did," I said, trying not to sound bitter—and failing. "Left me, left his son, left his business, left the state. If you're his friend, you would know that."

The man shifted his weight. He was tall, powerful without being bulky. He was wearing jeans, work boots, a navy blue flannel shirt layered over a T-shirt, and a brown leather jacket. He had a ball cap on his head, but he took it off and ran a hand through his hair, which was dark blond and worn long behind his ears. He was good-looking, if you liked men. Which, right now, I absolutely did not.

I had no use for men, especially good-looking ones. The only male I gave a shit about anymore was my son.

"I told you, I'm not his friend," the man—Damon—said. "We worked together."

So he was a Fed, then. He didn't look it. Terry was clean-cut, his hair always trimmed short and his jaw freshly shaved. This guy looked like he didn't even own a dress shirt, let alone a tie. "What did Terry tell you?" I asked him.

"That he needed someone to head up security at the bar he owned. Someone good."

I felt Jimmy, the bartender, staring at my back from behind the bar. We'd had problems lately—rowdy assholes, drunk guys bothering women, guys pissing in the alley next door, even an attempted break-in. I only knew all of this because Jimmy filled me in. Until two weeks ago, I had never run a bar in my life. The business was Terry's. Now, apparently, if I wanted to keep my head above water, I was the new boss.

Maybe we needed a security guy. I didn't really know. I *did* know I didn't want anything to do with this particular guy.

I shook my head. "He misled you, just like he misled all of us. Sorry you came all this way, but we don't need anyone."

"Don't you?" Damon asked.

I narrowed my eyes at him. I already had an avalanche of problems today—just like every day for the past two weeks— and I didn't need one more in the shape of a stranger with an attitude. "What is that supposed to mean?"

He looked around. "Can we talk in private?"

"Probably not."

"Trust me, you're going to want to hear what I have to say." He stepped forward and reached out, maybe to touch my arm, but when he saw the look in my eyes, he backed up. "Fine." Then he walked past me, around the bar as if he worked here every day, and disappeared into the back room.

What the hell? He was alone back there in my office— Terry's old office—with all of my paperwork and my computer.

And the bank statements. I hurried to follow him, giving Jimmy a look. "You couldn't have stopped him?"

"Was he really a Fed?" Jimmy asked. "Maybe you should hear him out."

It figured that the men, even though they'd just met, would stick together and gang up on me. I followed Damon into the office.

As soon as I was inside, he closed the door. That should have alarmed me, maybe. But I could walk back out if I wanted, and even though he outweighed me with muscle, Damon Blake didn't scare me. I wondered if he should.

Damon sat down on the chair across from the desk and crossed an ankle over his other knee. "All right, let's talk," he said.

"You have some nerve."

"Take a seat and give me some intel, starting with your name."

I was pissed off. I'd also had the worst two weeks of my life —furious, lonely, painful, heartbroken weeks. The heartbreak wasn't so much for Terry, who was an asshole, but for our son, Miles. At thirteen, he had already started to get in trouble, and his father leaving town wasn't helping.

So maybe that was why I sat down. Because for a second, talking to a stranger didn't sound so bad. "My name is Andie English."

Damon folded his hands in his lap. He had long legs in those jeans, which I could appreciate in some distant part of me that wasn't enraged. He was thin, though—maybe too thin, as if he'd been unwell recently. "You didn't take Terry's last name."

I shook my head. "Best decision I ever made, considering my lawyer is working on the divorce papers."

"So he lied to me when he said this bar was his. It's actually yours."

"Not exactly. This bar was Terry's thing. He wanted to buy it, he wanted to run it. I had nothing to do with it until he skipped town. But it's our main source of income, so if I want to keep eating, I have to keep it afloat myself."

"Did you have a job before Terry left?"

"I was a part-time freelance bookkeeper, and I raised our son."

He was watching me steadily. He had dark lashes around his gray eyes, but something about his look was cold and impersonal. "So until two weeks ago, you'd never run a bar before."

"No!" I almost shouted. "Why are we talking about this? Are you trying to be my therapist?"

That made a smile touch his lips. "Believe me, no one needs a therapist more than I do. I just find it diverting to talk about your problems instead of mine."

I leaned back in the old desk chair, making it creak. "What are your problems?"

"Like I say, we'll talk about them later. Or never. Let's get back to you, and the problems with this bar."

"I didn't say there were problems with the bar."

"Terry messaged me," he said, and his voice was low and chilled. For a second I could see the federal agent he'd been, dealing with very dangerous people on a regular basis. "We didn't know each other that well and we didn't particularly like each other all that much, but he still looked me up and asked me to come here. That wasn't a whim. He had a reason."

I bit my lip, then shrugged. "Sometimes it gets rowdy in here, I guess. Drunk guys. That's what they tell me."

"You haven't seen it yourself?"

"I don't hang out here in the evenings. I have a son at home to take care of. And I don't drink."

Damon's gaze was flatly disbelieving. "You own a bar, and you don't drink."

"I didn't ask to own a bar. I just ended up with one."

"Okay. So other than rowdy assholes, what else has been going on?"

I dropped my gaze to the messy desktop, with its pile of papers and its clunky old PC. "There was an attempted break-in. Two guys with baseball bats going for a window in the middle of the night. Luckily someone spotted them and called the police before they could get inside, but they ran off when they heard sirens coming. The cops didn't find them. I had to get the window replaced."

"Did the witness see their faces?"

"No. And now I've paid for the window because the place wasn't secure without it, and now the insurance company is giving me trouble with my claim. They say they're going to raise my premiums." I lifted one of the papers from the stack on the desk. "That's this problem, here. The top one on the pile of problems. Below it are complaints from suppliers that haven't been paid, a utility bill that's inexplicably high, and a letter from a lawyer threatening to sue Terry for sexual harassment of a former waitress here. Do you want me to go on?"

He shook his head, his gaze on the pile of papers. There was a moment of quiet. This man didn't feel the need to talk nonstop.

Then he said, "I've spent the last eight years on the DEA. Before that, I was a drug dealer and a budding addict. I went straight, got clean, and joined the force. I spent my time under-cover, working to take down some of the biggest dealers in the country, before I got shot twice in a raid. Now I'm not on the force anymore."

I felt my jaw drop as he spoke. When he finished, I was speechless.

"I'm telling you this so that you know who I am," Damon went on. "You can do a background check. The Feds gave me a severance, so I'm not desperate for money, but I need some-thing to do. It's why I came here when Terry offered the job. I don't want to sit around, feeling useless, when I'm not even forty. I don't have a wife or kids, and right now I don't even have a home. I'm not leaving Salt Springs, because I have nowhere else to go. So, you may as well make use of me."

"Make use of you how?" I asked. That sounded vaguely dirty, but he didn't seem to notice.

"There's no security system in this place," Damon said. "There are no cameras. I'm willing to bet there is no safe. This office has a shit lock on the door. Who else has access to it?" I opened my mouth, but he went on before I could answer. "I just walked in here with no problem, and no one stopped me. I saw a cash box behind the bar that looked like it came from a dollar store. And I haven't looked at that computer, but I'll bet money it doesn't have a security password."

A breath hushed out of my throat. I didn't want to admit he was right. The computer didn't have a password.

"Frankly, if I was looking to rob someone, this is the first place I'd pick," Damon said. "It's fucking perfect."

I closed my eyes, willing the stress and panic down. *I'm trying!* I wanted to shout. *I don't know what I'm doing! This isn't fair!*

But guess what? Life wasn't fair. It was a cliché, but it was true. I had a son to raise, and the Wild Wild West—as ridicu-lous as it was—was the only means to do it. At least, until I could think of something else.

"What are you suggesting?" I asked him, my voice hoarse.

"Hire me," he said.

I opened my eyes. "Damon, I don't even think I can afford to pay you."

A flicker of something I couldn't read crossed his eyes, and then they went cold again. "Give me four weeks," he said. "Pay me at the end of it if you think I've earned it."

I made a disbelieving sound. He had to be putting me on. "You're offering to work for free?"

"I'm offering to defer my paycheck," he shot back. "We can call it a trial period."

I shook my head. "I don't even know you. I just met you. I can't decide this right now. Maybe it's you who's going to rob me blind."

Instead of being offended, Damon nodded. "Now you're using your brain." He stood up, took a scrap of paper and a pen from the edge of the desk, and wrote a number on it. "Here's my cell. I'll be back here tomorrow at one. Use the time to look me up. I wouldn't trust me, either." He left the paper on the desk and turned to leave.

"Where are you going?" I asked him.

"To find an apartment," he said. "I'm going to spend the next four weeks getting some mountain air."

THREE

Andie

I DIDN'T WASTE much time. After the door closed behind Damon Blake's—admittedly rather nice—jean-clad ass, I picked up my cell phone. But I didn't call a service that does background checks. I called my dad.

"Hi honey," he said when he answered. "What's up?"

I immediately felt a few degrees of tension leave my neck and shoulders. My dad had been the county sheriff until three years ago, when bad health caused him to retire. He and I had always had a complicated relationship, because he hated Terry and had advised me not to marry him when I got pregnant by mistake. *You're going to regret this forever,* he'd said to me on my wedding day. *Your mother would hate him, too.* That hadn't gone over well, and we were estranged for a long time. The fact that Dad was right had been a hard pill to swallow.

But despite our rocky road, he was still my dad. He was also Miles's grandfather, and in his retirement he'd started to spend more time with my son. They had a relationship that was special to them both, and I respected that. God knew Miles needed a grown man in his life who wasn't his no-good father.

"Dad, do you still have access to background checks?" I asked.

"I can make some calls. Why? Someone bothering you?"

"No, nothing like that. I just—" I paused. Dad wouldn't understand that I was thinking about hiring a total stranger to take over security for the bar—a man who knew Terry, at that. He'd think I was on the verge of doing something stupid, just like when I'd gotten knocked up and then married. "I'm thinking of hiring someone and I want to be sure of him first."

"Why? What's his problem?"

"No problem. I'm just being careful."

"Sure, I get that. Send me a copy of his ID and his social security number, and I'll do a check."

Oh, right. "I don't have those yet. Just a name."

"You're thinking of hiring someone and you didn't ask for his ID? Andie, you know better than that."

I closed my eyes. Conversations with my dad were always like this. "It's just an idea at the moment."

"What are you hiring for? I thought Terry had all the staff he needed at the bar."

"I'm thinking of adding someone."

"That seems like an expense."

I tried not to shout. "I can handle it. If you don't want to do it, it's okay. I'll hire a service."

"And overpay? It sounds like you're not being very careful with money. You'll have to make some changes if you want to keep the bar afloat."

Was that a stress headache crawling up the back of my skull, or just the headache I'd had every day for the past two weeks? It was hard to tell. "Fine," I gritted out. "Don't do it. It doesn't matter."

"Of course I'll do it." He actually sounded surprised. "Jeez, you're touchy today."

I wished I hadn't called. I should have just accepted Damon Blake's story at face value, hired him on the spot, and let him rob and possibly kill me. That sounded easier than this. "I just have a name," I said again.

"Where was he born?"

"I have no idea."

Dad sighed, as if everyone should ask everyone where they were born. "I'll see what I can do."

I gave him Damon's name and ended the call, reassuring him that everything was fine, just fine. When I hung up, I stared at the pile of problems on my desk, trying not to panic. It was nearly five, and I needed to get home to Miles.

A few months ago, Miles had campaigned to start riding his bike to school instead of taking the school bus. He was thirteen, not a baby anymore, and the bike ride was only fifteen minutes. He'd get fresh air and exercise every day, he said, but really what he wanted was some freedom. Terry had been mostly checked out, so of course the decision had fallen to me. If I said yes and something bad happened to Miles, I was a bad mother. If I said no, I was smothering him as he sought his independence.

I'd said yes, on the condition that he get home no later than four thirty every day. Since I worked from home at the time, it was easy for me to monitor. But since Terry left, I had been forced to work at the Wild Wild West—or the Wild, as everyone called it for short. I was no longer home by four each day, which meant that Miles was home unsupervised until I got there.

We'd had another blowout about this. Miles said he was

perfectly capable of making himself a peanut butter sandwich and playing video games home alone until I got home. Logically I knew he was right, but I couldn't shake the feeling that I was missing something. Was Miles lying to me? Was he coming home later because I wasn't there? What kind of horrific parent was I to suspect my sweet thirteen-year-old boy? Was I paranoid? Why did this simple problem make me feel like my family was falling apart no matter how hard I worked to keep it together?

Was I actually going crazy? It felt like it sometimes.

In the end, I'd had no choice but to agree to Miles's terms. I had to be at the Wild every day, and I couldn't be home watching his every move. I was a single mother now. That was reality.

Still, it was nearly five, and my son could be murdered or on drugs right this minute. Also, I had to cook dinner. I needed to get home. I didn't like being at the Wild too late anyway, because the later it got, the wilder it got. I didn't like being at the bar at night.

Which is probably why you need to hire a security guy. Because you don't feel safe in your own bar.

I tried not to think about it as I put on my jean jacket and picked up my purse. The pile of problems would be here tomorrow; God knew it wasn't going anywhere.

Damon had said he was going to find an apartment. I wondered if he'd succeeded. He'd probably end up at a motel or at an AirBnB. There were a lot of listings in Salt Springs, I knew, but the expense would add up fast. Maybe he'd get discouraged and decide to leave town after all. And why was I thinking about Damon Blake and his scruffy jaw at all? Why was I wondering what his story was, what the problems were that he wasn't going to tell me about? He was none of my business.

I said goodnight to Jimmy, who gave me a wave. One of the regulars at the bar, already a few drinks in, also waved at me. "Have a drink with me!" he called out.

I ignored him and headed for the door. Since Terry had left, some guys thought it was open season for me. They were wrong.

WHEN I GOT HOME, Miles, as promised, was playing a video game in the living room. Next to him was a Coke and an open bag of chips.

"Where did you get those?" I asked him. I wasn't a health freak, but I didn't buy Coke or chips to keep in the house. If I did, Miles would eat nothing else.

He shrugged. "Bought them with my allowance."

I frowned, deciding whether to lecture Miles on the proper use of his allowance versus spending it on junk food. But he'd come home on time, and I didn't want to rock the boat. "Don't eat too much," I said, unable to help the mom in me. "I'm about to cook dinner."

My son rolled his eyes, because no matter what, he was always able to eat more food. He didn't bother to answer me.

I changed my clothes—my work clothes always smelled like a bar, no matter how much I ventilated the Wild during the day —and went to the kitchen to start on dinner. Even though I was an overworked, stressed-out, newly single mom, I felt a pang of actual happiness as I cooked rice and chopped vegetables, the sound of my son's video games in the next room. Things had been so tense with Terry here—or with Terry not here, as he usually wasn't this time of day. Until we split up, I hadn't realized how much mental energy I'd spent wondering where Terry was and why he never told me anything. I'd been simmering with useless anger that sometimes boiled over into arguments with him. To tell the truth, I'd suspected he was cheating well before he took off with his girlfriend, but I hadn't wanted to know the truth. I'd thought about Miles and my father's judgments and I'd swept my suspicions under the rug.

I'd stopped having sex with Terry, though. It was well over a year since I'd let him touch me, which was the source of even more fighting. I'd lived in a shadowy half-existence, not really married but too cowardly to leave, just existing from one day to the next to raise my son and pay the next round of bills. I hadn't been living at all.

And then Terry had dumped me, and the worst possible thing had happened after all. Miles lost his father, I was humiliated in front of everyone, and my own father had had plenty to say about my bad choices. *I told you that man was no good* was his favorite refrain. All I could think was, *If I had just divorced Terry years ago, I could have gotten all of this over with.*

But it was done now. Terry was gone, my embarrassment was public, and now it was just Miles and me. I was furious with Terry, but in moments like this I didn't even think about him. I thought about how peaceful it was not to wonder where my so-called husband was and what he was doing. Or who he was doing.

I was finished with men. Absolutely, completely finished. I didn't want the stress, the complication, or the emotion of a man in my life. I had Miles to think about, and he had been disrupted enough without me bringing someone new into his life.

Damon Blake flashed through my thoughts again, those gray eyes that could be so cold but were so intelligent at the same time. The way his hair curled against his neck. His legs in those jeans. No, I definitely wasn't thinking of him in that way.

After meeting him once, I already knew that Damon would be more stress and complication than I ever wanted to see again.

Besides, he could be a murderer just released from prison.

I cooked dinner for Miles and me, and didn't admit to myself that I really hoped he wasn't.

FOUR

Damon

WHAT THE HELL was the matter with this town?

The first apartment I looked at was being sublet by a guy who was—he was very frank about it—going into rehab. "It isn't fair, man," he said to me, shaking his head. "My ex-wife says I have to get clean if I want to see the kids again. I just want to live my life, you know?"

I nodded as if this made sense to me, and then I went and looked at a different place. This one was the guest house on a huge property that also contained a house, a barn, and such a large crop of weed that the smell wafted over us on the breeze. "You steal weed, I'll kick you out," the woman renting the place warned me. "That's my only condition."

I nodded and kept looking. Maybe I was a jaded ex-DEA agent, but that place looked like an excellent spot to hide a body. And I had no objection to weed, but I didn't need to smell it in my sleep.

The third place I looked at was on the second floor of an old duplex. The man living on the first floor was the owner, and he was definitely over eighty, though he was wiry and tough. "You a cop?" he asked me, staring at me with narrowed eyes as we stood in the empty apartment.

He had a good eye, I'd give him that. "I was."

"You don't look like a beat cop," he said. "A detective, more like."

"Fed," I corrected him, shrugging. I may as well tell the truth. "Former DEA."

That made his eyes go wide, and then he looked shifty. "I don't do drugs," he said, just a shade too loud.

I nodded. "Sure. Sure you don't."

"I mean it. Okay, I'll admit—I did in my younger days. Maybe quite a bit. Shrooms, acid. Not the hard stuff. Hell, I was young. It was a different time."

This wasn't an unusual reaction. When people I met heard I was with the DEA, they tended to volunteer their entire drug history without me asking. It always ended with the same sentence: *But not now. I don't do any of that now.* Like clockwork. No one ever did *anything* now.

I didn't actually care about anyone's drug history, and I definitely didn't care that this guy did shrooms fifty years ago. But people always assumed.

"Okay," I said.

"I smoke some weed every once in a while to take the edge off," the guy went on as if I was cracking down on him in the interview room. "Hell, I'm eighty-two and it's legal. Are we going to have a problem?"

"No, we're not going to have a problem." I was getting impatient. I needed somewhere to sleep. "I'm not with the DEA anymore, and even if I was, I wouldn't care. I just want an apartment. Do you want me to rent it or not?"

The man narrowed his eyes at me. "You got first and last months' rent?"

"Yes." The rent in Salt Springs was cheap, at least compared to everywhere else I'd lived.

"Damage deposit?"

"Sure."

"Fine then. You can rent it. Don't stomp too hard on the floorboards, because I can hear you. I go to bed at nine, so I don't want any noise after that. I listen to the Road Kings on my stereo sometimes because they're my favorite band. I saw them live seven times before they broke up." He held out a bony hand. "My name's Carl. Go write me a check."

I moved in.

Salt Springs seemed to be full of eccentrics and former hippies, various wanderers and misfits. It was perfect for me, except for the drugs. Aside from the fact that I'd been DEA, I didn't do drugs and I didn't grow them. I didn't buy or sell them. I didn't even drink. I might be the soberest guy in town.

I didn't own any furniture, so I was happy that the apartment came with a bed, a rickety kitchen table, and an old sofa. The spring wind whistled in the edges of the windows. When I stepped out the back door, I found a small deck that overlooked an incredible view of the mountains in the distance. There was no scent of weed. For the first time I thought that a few weeks in Colorado might actually be healthy for me.

Then I smoked a cigarette.

I took a shower, crawled into the bed, and fell immediately into a dreamless sleep.

ANDIE ENGLISH DIDN'T CALL me. I spent the next morning doing what I should have done in the first place:

sitting at my laptop, looking up Terry, this town, and a bar called the Wild Wild West.

This town was definitely weird, known for its artsy shops and its population of hippies of all ages. It was also a college town, and the hippies and the college kids didn't mix. The crime rate was average, leaning heavily toward charges of drunkenness by the college kids and possession of the substances that were still illegal by everyone else. It all seemed like good, clean fun, but my years in the DEA had put my senses on alert.

I found Terry easily on his Facebook page. I wasn't on social media myself, but I had an alias I used on Facebook when I needed to research someone for work. I had ways of using subterfuge to get information, but I didn't need to do that for Terry. His page was public and he had posted pictures of him and his new girlfriend—who was much younger than him, of course—in Key West. The girlfriend had a tiny bathing suit on, because Terry was the kind of guy who would post pictures of his girlfriend in a tiny bathing suit on a public Facebook page. In one picture, she was waterskiing and laughing while Terry drove a boat, like they were taking stock photos.

"What a knob," I said out loud, scrolling through the page. He had left Andie and his own kid for this? What was wrong with him? Andie was a lot better-looking, with her dark curls and her killer figure. Even her scowl, which she'd directed at me the entire time I talked to her, was sexy.

Not that I would act on anything I was thinking. Andie gave out a "fuck off" vibe, and I didn't blame her. She'd been married to Terry the Knob, and then she'd been dumped by him. Any woman would be done with men after that.

I reached back in my memory, trying to remember Terry when I'd briefly worked with him. It had been on an op in New

Mexico. He did good work, but he was smug and pretty sure of himself. I remembered a night after it was over when everyone went out to celebrate at a bar. I'd done my usual thing on nights like that, which was to go for the first hour only and drink soda water, bailing when people started to get drunk. That way I avoided temptation, but I also avoided the inevitable drunk questions: "You mean you don't drink *at all?*" To which I would have no choice but to answer, "Yes, fuckwad, that's what being an addict in recovery means."

Terry, I remembered, drank harder than anyone that night. When I left, he was talking to a woman at the bar, the two of them deep in conversation. I'd assumed he'd gone home with her, and I hadn't cared, because I'd had no idea he was married. He'd never worn a ring.

Now I knew. Jesus, what a knob he was. I scrubbed my hand over my face, realizing I'd been working with a cheater. We weren't buddies, or even close, which again made me wonder why Terry had emailed me, offering me this job.

There was no way to avoid what my gut was telling me: Terry had an angle.

I didn't know what it was yet, but I would. I opened my email and shot a quick note to Terry. *Hey man, I got here, all is good. Your wife is hiring me at the bar.* I hit Send without any more detail than that, which would reel him in.

As for the Wild Wild West bar, it had an outdated website advertising Friday night ladies' nights with two-dollar shots. Further searching told me that most people called it the Wild, the college kids mostly avoided it, and it was known as a place you could pick up someone or maybe score something illegal if you knew who to ask. In other words, it was shady.

I didn't like the idea of Andie running a place like that. She wasn't a shady woman. She probably didn't know half of what went on at the Wild, which made her vulnerable to danger.

She needed me. I only hoped she was smart enough to figure that out.

FIVE

Andie

DAMON'S BACKGROUND CHECKED OUT. I wasn't surprised, because for some reason I hadn't thought he was lying to me. I just had to be sure. After all, apparently I had terrible taste in men.

"He was a Fed," my dad told me, sounding suspicious when he called me with the results of his background check. "Probably a friend of Terry's. Why do you need a Fed working at the bar?"

"Maybe he'll keep some of the lowlifes out," I said. "You know the window got broken. It might be useful having him around."

"Terry was a Fed, and he never did screw-all," Dad grumbled. He never swore.

He was right. Terry had bought the bar when the old owner retired. He'd claimed he was going to turn the place around and make a success of it. I'd worried about the money, but after years taking down drug dealing scum, I'd figured Terry deserved to take a shot at a second career where he didn't put his life on the line every day. I'd backed him up and believed in him, made it work like a spouse was supposed to do.

And Terry, as my dad put it, hadn't done screw-all. He hadn't updated the bar, done any marketing, or even bought a new sign. The Wild made some profit because of its regulars, but it wasn't as much as it could be. Salt Springs was full of oddballs, but parts of it were slowly gentrifying with people moving from Denver for cheaper real estate, and we got more and more tourists every year. There were also a lot of college kids in town who never came here. The bar could have more customers, but Terry had never listened to my suggestions. Instead, he'd said that this was his project, one he needed to do alone—which meant *back off*.

Worse, he'd never let me look at the books. I was a professional bookkeeper, and it seemed like the easiest way to save money would be to let me do the books. But he hadn't. I'd never even seen the books, and since I took over, I hadn't actually *found* them.

It had only been two weeks. I tried not to think about that. The books would turn up, and when they did, I would go through them, and they would be fine.

I'm not in over my head, I thought as I got Miles off to school, alone on his bike, and got in my car to go to the Wild. *I'm not.*

Damon had said he would come back today, and I wondered if he actually would. Maybe he'd decided that Salt Springs wasn't his kind of place, and he'd left town already. Maybe he'd thought twice about working for a woman who was a bit bitchy because her life was falling apart. Weirdly, I hoped he would actually show. I wasn't sure how I would feel if he didn't.

Of course, I could simply call him. He'd left me his number. But I had too much pride to do that, and these days it felt like pride was all I had left.

Instead, I worked the morning with a weird sense of anticipation. The West wasn't open in the mornings, so it was a good time to do things like inventory and cleaning and office work that was best without interruptions. I was still going through the old computer in the office, trying to figure out where all the files were and how the bar was run. It was like trying to piece together a mystery after someone has died—except that Terry wasn't dead, he was in Florida with the woman he'd been sleeping with instead of me. I wasn't going to call him and ask him about suppliers or tax returns. I'd rather die.

When it got close to the time that Damon was supposed to show up, I got too distracted to work. We were open by then, and Jimmy was behind the bar, serving a few daytime regulars. I did a wander through the main bar, which I didn't often do, thinking about what Damon had said about security. The cash box really *did* look like it came from a dollar store. We really didn't have any security system, any cameras, or any wiring for it. What the hell had Terry been thinking?

I was standing next to the bar, staring up at a spot in the corner where a camera might go, when I heard a familiar voice at my shoulder. "What are you looking at?"

I jumped. It was Damon, and he was right next to me, so close I could catch a whiff of his scent. I turned and looked at him. "What?"

He pointed to the spot on the ceiling. "What's so interesting?" he asked. He was wearing jeans and work boots again, but he was wearing a clean white Henley beneath the brown leather jacket. He'd left off the baseball cap, and his dark blond hair looked soft and clean. The beard on his jaw was neat and trimmed close to his skin. He looked at me curiously from those gray eyes, rimmed with dark lashes.

"Um," I said, stupid for a second. It was the eyes, maybe. Or the scent, which was clean male skin mixed with leather. Or just the presence of him, so close. His presence hadn't hit me like this yesterday. When was the last time a man made me stupid? I couldn't remember.

Damon raised his eyebrows, waiting. And oblivious.

I gathered myself. "I'm looking for spots where cameras would go. You're right, this place doesn't have any."

Damon nodded. "Does that mean I'm hired?"

It took a second for me to form the words, even though I'd already decided. It was just so, so hard to ask for help. So goddamned hard. "If you're still willing to work four weeks as a trial, then yes," I ground out.

The corner of his mouth twitched, as if he had an idea of what that sentence had cost me. "I guess that means you looked me up."

I shrugged. "You check out well enough."

"Good. I'll start right now."

"Fine." Why did that sound like a challenge? I cast my mind around, trying to think of what came next, now that Damon was actually working for me. "How about you write up a list of your security suggestions?"

He actually rolled his eyes, as if he was Miles. "Really? A list?"

"Yes, a list." I straightened my spine and looked him in the eyes. I'd thought that sounded pretty good. "Make a list, and when I get back, we'll go over it and cost out each suggestion so I can make a budget. You can use the office."

"When you get back? Where are you going?"

"I've set up a series of meetings with our suppliers. The first one is this afternoon. I'm meeting with our whiskey supplier in Denver." I needed to meet our suppliers in person. I also needed to discuss with them the stack of late and unpaid invoices in the office. It wasn't going to be fun, but I was ready for it. We had to keep the booze coming into the Wild.

"That's a good idea," Damon said. "I'll come with you."

I frowned at him. "No, you won't."

"Yes, I will."

We stared each other down, and then I said, "You've only been employed by me for two minutes, and already you don't take direction very well."

"I never said I'd take direction," Damon said, and something about his voice made the sentence sound dirty. Was that intentional? Or did he just sound dirty all the time?

Or was it me that was dirty?

No, it definitely wasn't me. I was a bookkeeper, for God's sake. And a mom. And an ex-wife who was absolutely done with men. "There's no reason for you to come with me," I argued.

Those gray eyes softened a little. "Andie. If I come with you, I can learn more about how this place runs. What kind of relationships Terry had with his suppliers, that kind of thing. It will help me do my job."

I hesitated. In fact, I'd been sort of dreading the drive to Denver to deal with this alone. Lately, it felt like I'd been dealing with everything alone. Probably because I had.

Truth be told, I'd been dealing with everything alone for a long time before Terry had even left.

I crumbled. Just an inch.

"We'll take my car and I'll drive," I said, not willing to give in completely.

Damon smiled, and then he shrugged. "Fine with me."

SIX

Andie

DAMON WAS quiet as we drove. It was an easy silence, not awkward. At least, not awkward on his part. I found myself getting more and more tense, my shoulders tightening, my legs wanting to move. He seemed surprisingly large in my small, sensible Tercel. Damon's body was deceptive. He was too thin, probably because of his injuries, but in close quarters you realized just how tall and powerful he was. Or at least I did.

Finally, unable to take the lack of conversation any longer, I blurted out the first thing that came to mind. "How are you feeling?"

Damon glanced my way, surprised. "What?"

"How are you feeling? You said you got shot twice before you left the DEA. That must have been hard."

Now I sounded like an idiot. *That must have been hard?* As Miles would say: No shit, Sherlock.

"I'm all right," Damon said evenly. "The bullets hit me in

the upper chest. Right side. They thought I would lose a lung, but I didn't. It damaged my scapula, which was the most painful part after surgery. It took months to heal."

Jesus. I couldn't imagine feeling two bullets hit me. It must have been terrifying. "Didn't you get shot during a raid? Tell me they caught the guys, at least."

"Yeah, they caught the guys." There was a smile in his voice. "That was the whole idea. But that was the end for me as a Fed. I was out."

"Do you still have pain?" I asked.

"Sometimes, yes. Usually at night."

"They have pills for that."

My attempt at wit fell flat when he said, "I can't take opiates. I'm an addict."

"Oh. Right. You said that." I tried not to fidget in my seat. He was too close, and I was having some kind of reaction to him, a reaction I wasn't used to. It made my skin feel sensitive and my blood pump faster. "Are you going to explain to me how a guy who was an addict and a drug dealer ended up in the DEA?"

"You have a lot of questions."

I shrugged. "We're stuck in this car together, in traffic. We have time."

We were, indeed, in traffic. I inched the car along for a moment as Damon seemed to think about my question.

"I never got caught," he said. "Using or dealing, I mean. You can't become a Fed if you have a criminal record."

"Okay, so you weren't that bad, then."

He shook his head. "I broke the law plenty. I just didn't get nailed for it. That's the only difference between me and one of the guys I put away."

"Okay, then. But something must have happened. Something that turned you off the path of a life of crime and onto the path of law enforcement."

He frowned at me. "Are you sure you're a bookkeeper? You said I sounded like a therapist, but now *you* sound like one."

I laughed. "If I had an hour to myself and even a little bit of money, I'd probably go to one. It couldn't make things worse, right?"

Damon drummed his fingers on his knee. "Therapy never did much for me," he said. "I already know my childhood sucked."

Yeah, this guy was trouble. Bad childhood, drugs, bullet holes. Definitely not my type—not that I was thinking about him that way. If I ever wanted a man again—which was never—I'd want the square, upstanding, rule-following type. A guy with a proper career, a savings account, and a 401(k). Someone who gave me missionary position orgasms every Friday night and could help guide Miles onto a proper career path. And why was I thinking about this right now? Damon and I weren't dating. He was just my security guard.

"What are you thinking about?" Damon asked. "I can see the wheels turning in your head."

I cleared my throat, unwilling to admit I'd been thinking about how I was definitely not dating him. "I was thinking about how you didn't answer the question. What changed your path from drug dealing to the DEA?"

"I think this is our exit."

Shit, he was right. I signaled and frantically changed lanes. I didn't do a lot of freeway driving, and I wasn't used to it. I got honked at as I made the exit.

I had given Damon the address of the whiskey warehouse, and he used his phone to navigate us there. We were on the outskirts of Denver, in an industrial park made up of ugly concrete warehouses and bleak parking lots. When we pulled up and parked at Sheffer Whiskey, Damon's fingers were drumming on his thigh again, as if he was restless.

"We're a few minutes early," I said as I turned off the car in relief.

"Good." Damon got out of the car, reaching into the inside pocket of his leather coat as he unfolded his long, jean-clad legs and got out.

I got out, too, and saw that he had pulled out a pack of cigarettes. He tucked one between his lips and felt in his pockets for a lighter.

"Hey," I said, the word springing from me before I could think twice. "No smoking."

He paused, raising his eyebrows skeptically and looking around. He took the cigarette from his lips. "No smoking in this parking lot?"

I opened my mouth, trying to think of what to say. The words had been an impulse, because the sight of him about to light up had upset me. I couldn't have said why. Plenty of the old-timers at the Wild smoked until their teeth were yellow and their skin was like old shoe leather.

Maybe that was why.

"No smoking while you work for me," I said.

It was a complete overstep, a nosy request. It hung there in the air between us.

Damon's gaze was a combination of surprised and cold. "Did you just say I can't smoke if I work for you?"

He was intimidating, but there was nothing to do but double down. "Yes. I don't like the smell. It makes me queasy. Plus, it's bad for you."

"It's *bad* for me?" Damon couldn't quite believe what I was saying.

I couldn't either, but the more I dug my heels in, the more I was behind the idea. I really didn't like that Damon smoked.

"Yes, it's bad for you. Deadly, actually. You just got shot twice, Damon. You almost died. Don't you want to look after your health?"

"What I want," he replied flatly, "is to smoke this cigarette."

"Nope." I shook my head. "Not while you work for me."

He sighed. "Andie, you own a bar."

"I don't let anyone smoke in the Wild, either. The smokers have to go outside. Even if it's snowing or raining."

We stood there in a standoff in a parking lot. I knew I was asking for something crazy, but I also knew I was right. He shouldn't be smoking. I kept my chin up and kept my gaze on his without looking away.

He was a grown man, one I barely knew. One who outweighed me, gunshot wounds or no gunshot wounds. But after a reluctant pause, he put the cigarette back in the pack. "Only while I work for you," he said.

I nodded. "That sounds fair. Four weeks. You can quit for four weeks. Right?"

"Sure." He moved to put the pack into his coat pocket again. "No problem."

I held out my hand before he could put the pack away. "It's easier if you give them to me."

"Jesus," he said in a low, annoyed voice. But he gave me the pack.

I shoved the cigarettes into my purse, not sure what to do with them now that I had them. There wasn't a garbage can nearby. I couldn't quite believe he'd agreed to that. "We're on time now," I said. "Let's go in."

SEVEN

Damon

THE SHEFFER WHISKEY guy didn't like me. He was fifty-ish, with thinning hair and a mild paunch, the kind of guy that is a dime a dozen. I knew instantly that he likely had two kids he mostly ignored, he liked to golf, and when he was alone with his buddies they made off-color jokes and complained about how "you can't say anything anymore." He had expected a meeting with just Andie, who was hot and single. He was probably curious because she was Terry's ex and he wondered if he could flirt with her, since she was newly divorced. Instead, he not only got Andie, he got me.

And apparently I'd just quit smoking, so I wasn't in the mood for his shit.

We were sitting in his office after he'd given us a quick tour of the facilities. Andie had nodded politely as the guy—his name was Dave—talked on and on, though I knew she didn't drink. Dave would take her nods as encouragement and lean closer to her, smiling as he talked. Then he'd catch sight of me and he'd back away again.

"It's crazy, what happened with Terry," Dave said now, shaking his head as he sat in the chair behind his desk. "Just crazy."

Andie's voice got decidedly frosty at the mention of Terry. "Yes," she said. "Crazy."

"I mean, we did business for years. He seemed like a standup guy. We even went golfing together."

Bingo, I thought.

"Can't believe he just up and left town." Dave kept talking, unaware that he was pissing Andie off.

"Yes, well." Andie opened the messenger bag she'd brought and pulled out some papers. "I've been going through the accounts, and I've found a few things." She cleared her throat. "It seems we owe you money."

"Do you?" Dave's eyebrows went up. "The Wild was always up to date with the accounts."

"I'm still figuring everything out." Andie held up an invoice. "From what I can tell, this one from last month wasn't paid. And this one here," she pulled out another paper, "doesn't have a date on it, but it doesn't look paid either. It's a little unclear what this one is for."

"I'm sure it's fine." Dave waved a hand, dismissive, and then he smiled. "We're probably up to date. Terry and I didn't discuss that stuff much, to be honest. We had more of a hand-shake relationship, you might say."

"A handshake relationship?" Andie tucked a lock of hair behind her ear. I was seated in the chair next to hers, silent. It was Andie's job to handle the meeting. I was just the muscle.

"Sure," Dave said. "We'd ship to the Wild, and Terry and I would let the accountants worry about the details and such. Often, I'd make the delivery myself, and then he and I would

sit in his office and sample the goods, if you know what I mean."
He grinned again. "You and I can have the same relationship, if
you like. I think it would be mutually beneficial."

"Would it?" I asked, the first time I'd spoken.

Dave looked at me, and the smile faded from his face.

Andie seemed not to notice the tension between Dave and
me. She leaned forward in her chair. "So your accountant
might know whether these invoices are paid? They might be
able to tell me what this invoice is for?"

"Ah, my accountant is off sick today, I think," Dave said,
pulling his gaze off me and back to her.

"That's too bad. Can you give me their phone number? Or
their email? The only contact info I could find in Terry's
papers was yours."

Dave scratched the back of his neck. "Well sure, Andie—
may I call you Andie? I can send you whatever you want over
email. I'll find the info and send it when my accountant is back
in the office." He smiled at her again. "In the meantime, would
you like a sample? Since you came all this way."

Andie levelled a glare at him. "I *drove*," she said. "It's the
middle of the afternoon. I can't drink whiskey while I'm here,
and I don't drink anyway. What I need is—"

"What you need is to calm down," Dave said.

The words came out harsh, belying his shit-eating grin.
There was a second of silence in the office, thick and menacing.
I could take this guy, I thought, my instincts kicking in. *Easy*.
My muscles tensed.

Then Dave laughed. "You're obviously new to the business,
Andie," he said jovially. "We don't take things so seriously here.
It's about relationships, and if we want to take a little product-
testing break during the workday, we let ourselves cut loose. Do
you see what I'm saying?"

Andie looked shaken, her confidence thrown. Give her

some invoices and a list, and she was in her element, but she wasn't in her element here. I was suddenly glad I'd come.

"I'm just trying to square things," she said, her tone softer than before. "I don't want our relationship with our vendors to go sour."

"There's no worry about that." Dave pushed his chair back and stood. "Our relationship with the Wild is as good as ever, Terry or no Terry. And as much as I liked him, I have to say you're easier on the eyes." He winked at her and held out his hand to shake.

Andie paused, then pushed her chair back as well. "Okay, thank you." She shook his hand.

He didn't shake mine. I didn't offer.

EIGHT

Damon

WHEN WE GOT BACK to the car, I held out my hand and said, "Give me the keys. I'll drive."

"Why?" Andie glared at me, a red flush of anger on her cheekbones. "You know what? I think I've had enough of men and their idiotic attitudes today. What a load of bullshit. You think you should drive just because you have a dick? Get over yourself."

Well. She was sexy when she was mad, but I kept that thought to myself. "I'm offering to drive because I can hear your cell phone going off nonstop in your purse. You probably need to answer some calls and emails."

She pressed her lips together, her skin still flushed. In the silence, the phone in her purse buzzed again, loudly.

I raised my eyebrows. "Come on," I offered. "My dick and I will drive you back to Salt Springs."

She hesitated again, then slapped her keys into my hand. "I hate men."

I shook my head. "Baby, after that meeting in there, I don't blame you one bit."

We got in the car. I put on my sunglasses, started the car, and got us the hell out of that depressing parking lot.

Andie pulled her phone from her purse and started scrolling through the messages and emails coming in. After she'd typed a few responses and we were back on the freeway, she lowered the phone and said, "So I wasn't hallucinating, right? That was bad back there."

She seemed to need to hear it, so I didn't mince words. "That guy was a piece of shit."

She sagged against her seat, some of the tension leaving her shoulders. "What was he doing, though? Did he think he was coming on to me?"

"If I wasn't there, he would absolutely have asked you out," I said.

"Terry was his friend. I'm Terry's ex. He left *two weeks* ago." She seemed incredulous.

"You're a hot, single woman, so you're fair game," I said. "That's how guys like that think. You have more vendor meetings set up?"

Andie blinked at me. "What? Yes. I have a meeting every afternoon this week."

"Fine. After meeting that guy, I've made a decision. I'm coming with you to every one."

Now she was getting mad again. "What for? To preserve my virtue? If one of these guys asks me out, I'm perfectly capable of saying no."

I noticed that she didn't even entertain the idea, and I approved. "It isn't to protect your virtue," I explained. "Aside from his chauvinist bullshit, something stunk about that guy.

The business might be legit, but there's no way he's completely on the up-and-up. I spent too many years dealing with guys like that, and I've seen it too many times. Something's rotten."

"Rotten how?" she asked. "The invoice thing is definitely weird. But what do you mean?"

"Well, for a light starter course, probably tax evasion," I said.

"Oh, God. The IRS?" Andie put a hand over her eyes. "The last thing I need is the IRS."

"That's one of the simpler possibilities," I said. "I haven't even gotten to the bad stuff yet."

"Don't tell me. Just don't."

I drummed my fingers on the steering wheel. I was jonesing for a cigarette. I'd smoked on and off since I was a teen, but it had gotten bad in the last six months. Something about getting shot made a guy revert to his bad habits, especially when he's recovering without opiate painkillers. I'd told myself that cigarettes were the lesser of two evils.

But Andie had told me to stop, and for some crazy reason, I had agreed. I was already getting jittery. It didn't help that with every day that passed I had more suspicion that something was very wrong, and that something had to do with Terry.

I had the feeling that Andie was in trouble. I just didn't know what kind.

Sure, it was a cliché. She was a gorgeous, sexy woman who needed my help, a damsel in distress. I'd come for this job for something to do, and now I could do a white knight act if I wanted—except for the fact that Andie didn't particularly want me around. She didn't even seem to like me. Hell, no one liked me. My own brother hadn't spoken to me for thirteen years, and neither had his fiancée. I didn't blame either of them. For most of my life so far, my biggest talent had been for making mistakes.

Staying in this job instead of getting the hell out of Salt Springs—and getting away from whatever trouble this was—was probably another mistake.

Andie had gone back to her phone, texting and replying to emails. Then she gave a heavy sigh and called someone.

"Where are you?" she asked when the other person answered. "What do you mean, last period was cancelled at school? Why?"

So it was her son, then. She hadn't told me anything about him, except that he existed. He was Terry's son, who Terry had abandoned when he left town. Poor kid. I didn't know how old he was, but he was obviously old enough to have a cell phone.

"You're going to Jonathan's house?" Andie said into the phone. "I suppose that's okay. How many other kids are going there? Are his parents home? Text me the address in case I need it." Some type of groaning on the other end. "Yes, Miles, you have to. Are you going to eat dinner there? What kind of takeout? Try to eat something healthy. Remember you're allergic to seafood."

She went on in this vein for a while. When she finally ended the call, I said, "Teenager?"

"Thirteen." Her voice was tense.

I glanced at her. Her gaze was fixed on the road ahead, and I could see her perfect profile. Dark eyes, those dark curls of hair, perfect skin that had no need for makeup. She really was a gorgeous woman. Terry was insane.

"He's probably fine," I said, trying to relax her. "He just wants to hang out with his friends. I did that a lot at that age." I left out the part about how I also scored weed at thirteen, snuck out of the house at three a.m., and threw empty beer bottles at passing cars, because she didn't need to hear that. I'd been a particularly bad kid, left to go wild. My dad had hit me and my mom didn't care, so I'd acted out.

"I worry," Andie said, the words coming out like a reluctant admission.

"Why?"

She shook her head, as if she wanted to drop the subject, even though she'd brought it up. "It'll blow over. He's unhappy and confused because Terry left. He has to, I don't know, work through it." She looked at me. "You don't have kids?"

I laughed. "Considering what a lousy father figure I'd be, that's for the best for everyone."

"You couldn't be much worse than Terry. His only method of parenting was to let me do the disciplining so that he could always be the good guy—until he left with his new girlfriend. Did you know he's only talked to Miles on the phone once since he left?" The words seemed to come in a wave, as if now that she'd started, she couldn't stop them. "I know it affects Miles, but he won't talk to me. Sometimes I think I should get him to see a child therapist, even though money is tight. Then I think it's only been two weeks, and maybe Miles just needs time to process the change. Maybe he doesn't need me micro-managing him? Is there something I should be doing, or not doing? I can't be home for him all the time because I have to run the Wild. I don't know if that means Miles is mad at me, too."

There was quiet. She seemed to be at the end of her outpouring of words. I knew nothing about how to handle any of this, so I cleared my throat. "Um, it sounds like raising a kid is pretty hard."

She laughed at my simplistic assessment of the situation. "Sorry I dumped all of that on you."

"Did it make you feel better?"

"A little, yes."

We were entering Salt Springs again. We would park at the Wild, and she'd take her car home. It'd get in my own car and go home, leave Andie English and her problems behind. I'd go back to the simple life of the single guy. Andie and Miles were none of my business.

Just like I liked it.

No ties. No complications.

I really, really wanted a cigarette.

NINE

Andie

MILES WASN'T HOME when I got home. He was still at
Jonathan's. He'd texted me Jonathan's address, so at least I had
that much. I decided to leave him alone with his friends for a
few hours.

The house was quiet as I stripped off my clothes and took a
shower. When was the last time I'd had the house to myself? It
was so rare. After my shower, still wrapped in a towel, I lay on
the bed, my eyes closed in a few decadent minutes of not
having to do anything at all. With Miles having dinner at his
friend's, I'd probably make a grilled cheese sandwich and grab a
pickle out of the jar in the fridge. That would be the extent of
my cooking tonight.

I let my thoughts spin back over my day, and then—let's be
honest—I let them land on Damon Blake. After spending a lot
of time in close quarters with him today, I could admit that he
was hot. Something about his quiet, badass competence was

sexy. It hadn't escaped me how he'd shut down Dave in that meeting with just two words: *Would it?* They were the only two words he'd needed to speak, and Dave had shut up instantly. It had been bossy and alpha, and I'd liked it.

He was rough around the edges, but he had those sexy gray eyes. He also moved with an easy, lethal grace, like someone who has had a lot of training. Terry had been DEA, and he never moved like that. He was nothing like Damon at all.

Damon had called me hot. *You're a hot, single woman,* he'd said, tossing the words out casually. But I'd never been called hot before, and definitely not by a man who looked like Damon did. And Terry's abandonment was still so new that I hadn't really thought of myself as single. A hot, single woman? Was that how he saw me?

Did Damon get a lot of women? He probably could if he tried. Was he a relationship guy, or a one-night-stand guy? Maybe some woman had broken his heart in the past, which was why he seemed closed off, like me. But with Damon, there was something simmering beneath the surface. I wondered what he was like in bed, what kind of sex he liked. Fast and hard? Or slow? Did he have some kind of kink he liked?

That thought gave me a shiver, a delicious thrill that moved through my body. It had been so long since I'd had a shiver like that. Years.

Terry had been only my second boyfriend. Yes, it was the truth: At thirty-five, I had only slept with two men. A woman's sexual exploration gets cut short when she gets unexpectedly pregnant and marries the baby's father. To me, my sex life with Terry had always seemed perfectly fine, considering we had such a rocky start. Pregnancy, childbirth, and caring for a baby are life-changing things, but they aren't exactly sexy.

Still, we'd had years since then to get it together, and I'd thought we had. We didn't have a sex life that was particularly wild or crazy, but it was as regular as we could make it, and usually we were both satisfied. Until the relationship had started going sour, and our sex life had gone sour along with it. Then it had died altogether, something I was thankful for now that I knew Terry was screwing God knew who.

So my overall experience with sex was pretty pathetic, but it hadn't mattered. Or so I believed until Terry left. I was a mother and a wife and a part-time bookkeeper, not a woman who devoted her life to wild sex. And since Terry left, I had been so buried in hurt and stress that I hadn't thought about sex at all.

But I was thinking about it now. In my few minutes alone on my bed, wrapped in a towel, my skin tingling, I was thinking about Damon Blake. I was thinking about what his hands would feel like on me. What his skin would taste like. I was wondering what turned him on.

It probably wasn't me. But there was no harm in wondering.

When was the last time I'd done anything just for myself? When was the last time I'd indulged in being a healthy adult woman with a sex drive? I didn't even own a vibrator—I was too worried Miles would find it, and Terry would have made fun of me. I didn't watch porn. I didn't even ogle any good-looking men I saw on the street, because I was a married woman. Now I'd missed all those years of ogling for nothing.

I was so pathetic I didn't even let my *thoughts* become selfish and sexy. Where had I been all this time?

What would it be like if Damon was in the room right now? If he unwrapped the towel from my body and let it fall open? I pictured his hands on my skin, moving over me, and I shivered again.

I was in the middle of a pleasant, very dirty fantasy—it involved Damon and me on a beach, at night, naked—when my cell phone rang. Assuming it was Miles, I reluctantly let the fantasy go and answered.

It wasn't Miles. It was Terry.

My lustful mood, the pleasant warm blood pulsing in my veins—all of it dissipated with the sound of his voice. "Hello, Andie."

"What do you want?" I asked him.

He sighed, as if I was being an unreasonable shrew. I knew that sigh; he'd used it in many of our fights over the years. "Well, I *was* just checking in. I thought we could have a civilized conversation."

"About what?" I sat up and realized I was still wearing only a towel. Even though Terry couldn't see me, I felt naked. I pulled back the bedcover and slipped under it to cover myself. "Did you sign the divorce papers?" I asked.

"Yeah, I did. My lawyer added an addendum. You have to sign that part back."

Alarm froze my spine. "An addendum? Saying what?"

"It transfers the ownership of the Wild from me to you."

This made no sense. I was running the Wild right now because Terry had left and there was no one else to do it, and I needed the money. I didn't own it and didn't plan to. "Why?" I asked him. "Why would you do that?"

"Because it's my job to *support* you," he said in that argumentative tone that drove me crazy. "I'm being *nice*."

"If you're being nice, send me money. Not a bar I don't have time to run."

"See, Andie, that's your problem," Terry said. "I saved up money to buy that bar, and I bought it. Now I'm giving it to you, for nothing. And you're *complaining*."

The back of my neck had gone tight, and my shoulders were tense. I hated—*hated*—this tone of his voice. He knew it. When he used this tone with me, which was often, it was because he wanted to make me mad. That way, when I flew off the handle, he could point to what a lunatic I was. *She goes crazy at the smallest thing! I can't say anything!*

I gritted my teeth and tried to sound calm. "Fine, I'll take a look at the addendum. Anything else?"

"Yeah. I got an email from Damon Blake. Seems like he finally turned up for the security job."

"Finally?" I asked. "When was he supposed to turn up?"

"*Weeks* ago." Terry was back to complaining again. "I mean, he was packaged out, what else did he have to do? But he took his sweet time. Anyway, I don't think you should hire him. Just tell him to get lost and send him on his way."

I blinked. "You think I shouldn't hire him?"

"Well, what do you need him for? Think about it for a minute, Andie. The Wild is doing just fine."

I had the beginnings of a headache starting behind my eyes. "If the Wild doesn't need a security guy, then why did *you* hire him?"

"It was an impulse. I felt kind of sorry for him. I thought I could give him something to do. But we don't need him. Just send him on his way. He shouldn't give you any trouble."

My mind spun. First of all, I hated that he'd used the word *we* when I was now running the Wild all alone. And secondly, Terry was really getting on my nerves. Which meant that whatever he wanted me to do, I suddenly wanted to do the opposite.

"I don't know," I said. "I feel good with a security guy there. I like him."

"You hired him?" Terry sounded amazed.

"Why not? We had that break-in. I don't want to deal with the drunks myself, or make Jimmy do it all the time. It seemed like a good idea."

"Andie. I know Blake better than you do. He has some things in his past that are definitely shady."

"I know. He told me about them. It doesn't bother me."

"It should, because he was a fucking drug dealer." Terry paused. "Wait a minute. Are you hot for him?"

I'd think that Terry was psychic, but this was just his usual refrain. He'd used it on me plenty of times when he wanted to make fun of me. *Why do you talk to the UPS guy so much? Are you hot for him? Why did you make small talk with the waiter? Are you hot for him, Andie? I bet you are. That's hilarious.*

According to Terry, it was always hilarious when I found a man attractive.

And suddenly, I was mad—really, really mad. I wanted to hurt Terry more than I ever had before. *Yes, I am hot for him!* I wanted to shout. *I've met him twice and he's nicer to me than you ever were! I want to fuck him for days, and I'll bet he's better in bed than you!*

But I had to keep control. The final papers weren't signed yet, and if Terry got it in his head that I was sleeping with someone new, he could make problems over the custody arrangement for Miles. Maybe he wouldn't get away with claiming I was an unfit mother, but he could put me through a lot of expensive misery if he tried.

"I'm not hot for anyone," I said calmly. "But I need help at the Wild, and Damon is willing to take the job. So I hired him. And since the Wild is my bar now, you don't get a say."

There was a long pause. "Fine," Terry said, as if *he* had needed to make a decision. The asshole. "Where's Miles? Put him on."

"He's at his friend Jonathan's right now, but I'll tell him you called. I'm sure he'll be happy about it. I'll have him call you when he gets home."

"Fine," Terry said again, and then he hung up.

When I put the phone down, my hands were shaking with rage. Not because of Terry's attitude, or because he'd made fun of me, or because he'd left me in the first place after too many final years of a lousy marriage that had stolen a precious part of my life.

No. I was angry because in that whole conversation, the very last thing Terry remembered to ask about was his son.

TEN

Damon

I DIDN'T GO STRAIGHT BACK to my weird apartment, where Carl, my elderly downstairs neighbor, was most likely playing the Road Kings. I was hungry, and I was restless, so I drove around Salt Springs looking for something to eat. I decided on a taco place and picked up tacos to take home. After a long haul recovering from my injuries, my appetite was finally starting to come back.

The sun had mostly set by the time I came out of the taco place, dinner in hand, and walked to my car. My gaze was drawn to the liquor store next door, lit up with a blue sign above the door: FINE WINES AND LIQUORS. I wasn't looking because I was tempted to have a drink. I was looking because there were two kids loitering outside who were definitely underage, and I recognized one of them.

It took a second for me to place the kid's face. It was the

same kid I'd seen in the gas station on my way into town, quietly shoplifting chips and soda. He was lanky, with a boyish face and light brown hair left to grow a little long. He wore jeans, a baggy gray sweatshirt, and black Chucks. He was standing with his hands in his pockets, talking to a kid a few years older than him who had acne on his cheeks.

I dropped the bag of tacos onto my passenger seat and got into my car, watching the kids from the corner of my eye. There was only one reason an underage kid would loiter outside a liquor store—I'd done it plenty of times myself at that age. Sure enough, a minute later a guy of about twenty came out of the store, a bag of purchases in his arm. The kids jumped to attention and followed the guy to a car, where they all got in. It was the same car I'd seen pull away from the gas station.

And here I was, in this shit position again. Should I do something? Did I actually care that some guy was buying liquor for underage kids? *It's none of your business, Blake. Let it go.*

Still, when you've spent as long in law enforcement as I had, you develop a gut sense of things. Buying liquor for kids might not be a world-ending crime, but I didn't like the look of that car. I just didn't.

I should just forget it and go home.

Fuck.

I started my car and followed in the direction the other car had gone. I'd give it exactly two minutes, and then I'd go on my way.

The car was stopped at a light a block up the road, and I stopped behind it. I could see five people in the car, maybe more. Music was blaring out of it at top volume, a heavy metal song I didn't recognize, all wild guitars and screaming vocals.

The light changed to green, and the driver of the car stomped on the gas, making the car jump forward. It screeched off, accelerating. A joyride. I just hoped the guy driving hadn't already started drinking.

Should I follow?

Jesus, Blake, give it a rest. Go home already.

I made a sedate right turn and headed back to my apartment, unwilling to admit that I'd used the oldest cop trick in the book: I'd memorized the license plate. When I got home, I typed the plate number into my notes app on my phone and saved it. I told myself to forget about it. Then I ate my tacos.

I WAS STILL restless after dinner. I wanted a cigarette, bad. Why the fuck had I agreed to quit? Oh, right, because Andie English had asked me, and I had the hots for her. Like if I quit smoking when she asked me, I'd actually have a chance.

No. There was no fucking chance. Not with her.

It was full dark now. I put my jacket back on and walked the few blocks to the closest drug store, where I picked up a package of nicotine patches. I'd never tried them before, but there was a first time for everything. Maybe if I stuck the whole package on my arm, the craving would go away.

Carl's apartment was dark and quiet now, and I tried not to stomp—as he put it—as I walked back up the stairs to my apartment. I dropped my coat on the sofa and pulled out my laptop. I'd had insomnia for as long as I could remember, and there was no way I would sleep. There was something wrong with this picture here in Salt Springs, and I needed to start digging.

I couldn't have said why I cared. Salt Springs wasn't my town. These weren't my people. I didn't have any people, unless you counted my brother, Alex. But our relationship had been too badly damaged too many years ago, and I wasn't sure there was anything that could be done about it now.

I didn't care about Salt Springs, or the Wild, or Terry, or anything that was going on here.

But Andie did.

I rubbed the bridge of my nose. Spending the day with her had gotten under my skin. I could admit it. Her fucking pride. The way she'd faced down Dave the creep without a whisper of intimidation. The way she didn't act like beautiful women usually did. That was probably Terry's doing. Terry had probably spent years making her feel like she wasn't beautiful, when in truth she was.

If I got Andie naked, I could make her feel beautiful. So, so fucking beautiful.

It was not going to happen.

Andie English wasn't going to give me the time of day, but she was in over her head. She'd admitted as much when she'd dumped her problems on me on the drive home. Andie was swimming as hard as she could, but it didn't matter, because somehow she was still sinking.

I couldn't bang her, but maybe I could help her.

I went to the Wild's terrible website, found the phone number, and called it.

"Wild," was the curt answer on the phone. It was the Kenny Rogers lookalike. His name was Jimmy. I had to try and remember that.

"Jimmy," I said. "It's Damon Blake, the security guy."

"Hey, brother."

"Hey. I'm at loose ends here. Do you need me to come in tonight?"

"Nope, it's dead as a doornail. Nothing I can't handle. But Thursdays, Fridays, and Saturdays can be bad. We should work out a schedule."

"Yeah, we can do that. I'll be in tomorrow and we can do it then. I don't mind bouncing the troublemakers."

"Hope you don't mind a few hostile locals and the occasional puke."

"I can handle it. Since it's so quiet, can you do me a favor?"

"Sure."

"List me a few of our main suppliers. I want to do a little research into how the place runs."

"Yeah, I know a few of them." He listed off four names. "Those are the ones I know of."

"That you know of?"

"I haven't worked here all that long."

This was news. "When did you start?"

"Three and a half weeks ago. I was working at another bar that closed down, so I applied here. Apparently the last guy got fired, so they were stuck with me."

"Uh huh," I said, making a note beneath the list of suppliers I'd taken down. "What was the last guy's name? Do you know?"

"Uh, Doug something. I saw his name on the schedule when I first started, before they took it off. Doug Gardiner, that's it." He spelled it. "Why do you ask? Are you going to check him out?"

I wasn't sure how much to tell this guy. "I might."

"I hope you do. Apparently a lot of the staff got fired within the last month. I know there's a lot of turnover in this business, but you work enough bars, you get a feeling for which places have a smell to them. You know?"

I was going to interview Jimmy tomorrow at length, because he had exactly the information I was looking for. But I couldn't do it properly over the phone in the middle of his shift. "I know what you mean," I told him. "When are you in tomorrow?"

He told me, and we set up a time. "If you do a check on me," he said before hanging up, "just ignore the spousal support thing. I'm behind on payments, but I'm trying to catch up."

We hung up and I looked at my notes, thinking. Then I tapped my laptop awake. Terry hadn't answered my email.

What are you up to, asshole? I wondered.

I pulled the laptop toward me and got to work.

ELEVEN

Andie

"LET'S DO SOMETHING THIS WEEKEND," I said to my son as I poured coffee into my travel mug the next morning. Miles was sitting at the kitchen table, quickly scarfing down Corn Flakes before going out the door.

"Like what?" he asked without looking up.

I shrugged. "The weather's nice. We could find somewhere to go for a hike. Or we could go to the movies."

He crunched another bite of cereal. He was in a phase where it almost hurt me to look at him, because his face was so clearly that of my baby and also that of a young man. He didn't look much like Terry, thank God. What Miles truly looked like was photos of my father when he was a teenager. And in his young days, my dad had been a looker.

But Miles was still growing into himself. He grew his hair too long and let it flop over his forehead and his face, and he often sat hunched over. Baggy sweatshirts were his favorite items of clothing. I wanted to fuss over him every time I saw him, but I also knew I needed to keep some distance. I didn't want to drive him further away.

"I can't," he said in response to my invitation. "I'm hanging out with Cindy this weekend."

I stood up straight, as if someone had zapped me with electricity. "Cindy? Excuse me? Who is Cindy?"

I sounded like a mom, but I couldn't help it. I *was* a mom.

Miles rolled his eyes, one of his favorite moves of late. "Mom, it isn't anything. It's just hanging out. She's with Trevor anyway. He'll be there."

This was not reassuring. "Your friends are dating? No one should be dating anyone. You're thirteen."

"People hang out, Mom." His tone was exasperated. "Anyway, Cindy is having some people over, so I'm going to go. We'll do the movies or whatever another time." He pushed his bowl away—nothing on earth would get him to rinse it in the sink—and stood up, hefting his backpack. "I have to go."

"Do you want me to drive you?" I asked, following him to the door. "I don't mind."

"You'll be late for work."

"So? I can be late for work. I'm the boss."

"I'll take my bike. It's fine."

"You have a dentist appointment on Friday."

"Kay. Bye."

He got on his bike and pedaled away, and I felt yet again like I was somehow failing. Who was Cindy? Who was Trevor? Who were their parents? Would there be adult supervision? Why didn't Miles tell me anything?

I couldn't blame him for his mood. When he'd come home from Jonathan's last night, he'd called his father back. Terry hadn't picked up the phone.

Miles had barely said a word as he hung up. He'd gone into his room and closed the door. He hadn't come out again.

I stood in the empty house, my mind racing. Miles had his own cell phone with internet disabled on it. He had a computer in his room, and Terry had installed parental controls so that Miles could look up things for homework and chat with his friends without being able to go to restricted websites. But what if Miles had somehow disabled the controls? How would I know? And was he really turning his homework in on time? Whenever I asked him about homework, he always told me everything was "fine."

I hated, *hated* that I was suspicious of my own son. Then again, I hadn't seen a report on his marks in quite a while. Miles had told me there wasn't a new one uploaded to the school's online system yet, and in the chaos of the past few weeks, I'd forgotten to look.

I walked upstairs and stood in front of the closed door to his bedroom. I put my hand on the knob. My own parents had let me have privacy in my room, so this was hard for me to contemplate. Then again, my parents had had strict disciplinary rules, and after my mom died when I was ten, my dad hadn't let me have my own phone or computer until I was sixteen. That was what happened when your dad was a sheriff and had seen his share of the bad things that can happen to kids in the world.

I hadn't gone on my first date until I was nineteen, which was why I was shocked at thirteen-year-olds dating. I had been raised pretty sheltered. Then I'd met Terry, and my lack of experience meant I got pregnant with Miles, and now here we were. So maybe it was better to be a sheltered kid—or maybe it wasn't.

"I hate this," I said out loud, and then I opened the door.

It looked like a boy's room. The bed wasn't made, there were clothes in messy piles, and there were a couple of chocolate bar wrappers on the floor. I hadn't given him the chocolate bars, but if chocolate bars were the worst thing Miles was into, I'd be a happy mother.

I stepped into the room and looked around, trying to touch as few things as possible, as if my son could dust for finger-prints. I crouched and looked under the bed—nothing. I opened a drawer of his dresser and saw only socks and under-wear. A couple of schoolbooks were tossed in a corner. I tapped the keyboard on the computer, but it didn't wake. So it was powered off, then.

Should I power it on? He probably had a password on it.

I was distracted from this problem when I caught sight of the wastebasket on the floor next to the computer desk. It was stuffed with papers. I fished the papers out.

On top was a history test. Miles had gotten a D.

I stared at the grade, stunned. This wasn't like Miles at all. He was a smart kid. He *knew* this stuff. We'd had a call from the teacher a month ago, but for some reason she'd called Terry instead of me. The teacher had said she was worried about Miles's grades and his "lack of focus." Terry told me he had handled it.

Oh, right. *Terry handled it.*

I left Miles's room and went downstairs to the home office, where I kept my laptop. I powered it up and logged into the school's online system. There was a new report card uploaded last week.

Miles had lied to me. Worse, his grades were all C's and D's. He'd never had grades this low before.

I was going to have to contact the school. I was going to have to set up a parent-teacher meeting. I was going to have to handle this.

Everything else would have to wait.

TWELVE

Andie

I DIDN'T GET to the Wild until noon. The early-shift bartender, Cory, was behind the bar, pouring drinks for the daytime regulars. "Where's Jimmy?" I asked him. It was Thursday, which was payday for a lot of people and almost as busy as Fridays and Saturdays. We usually had two staff in on Thursday afternoons.

Cory looked a little uneasy. He was thirty, with hair he dyed black for some reason I couldn't fathom. If he was going gray, he'd look perfectly fine. "He's in the office."

That didn't make sense. I trusted Jimmy, but what was he doing alone in the office? I circled behind the bar, turned the corner, and opened the office door.

Jimmy wasn't alone in the office. Damon Blake was sitting behind my desk, wearing a faded gray T-shirt. His longish brown hair was brushed back from his face. He had scruff on his jaw. His arms were lean, strong, and tan. Jimmy was sitting in the chair across from the desk, and both men were laughing. The laughter wound down when they saw me.

"Morning, boss," Damon said. He looked comfortable in that chair.

"It's afternoon," Jimmy pointed out.

Damon glanced at his watch, a leather one that gleamed on his masculine wrist. "So it is. Afternoon, boss."

I watched his forearm flex, and I was suddenly reminded that before I was distracted by Terry and then by the problem with Miles, I had fantasized about getting naked with Damon. I felt heat creep up my neck and I shifted my weight. I was wearing my usual jeans and ankle boots, topped with a loose black sweater. Was my makeup okay? Why was I suddenly self-conscious? This was stupid.

"What's the meeting all about?" I asked. "And why wasn't I invited?"

Damon didn't seem to notice my sharp tone. "Close the door," he said, motioning with his hand. "Jimmy, pull out that chair."

Jimmy did as he was told, pulling a second chair from where it sat against the wall. I should kick Damon out of the chair behind the desk, but that would look pretty stupid, since I didn't know what we were talking about. I sat down.

"I'm interviewing Jimmy," Damon explained, seeing how uneasy I was. "We needed somewhere private, so we came in here. We didn't want to use the employee break room, because we didn't want anyone listening."

"Why are you interviewing him?" I asked, momentarily stupid. "He already has the job."

"More like a police interview," Jimmy said. He sat up straighter in his chair. "We're going over how things work at the Wild, some of the stuff that has gone on recently. That kind of thing."

Damon watched me steadily with his gray eyes as Jimmy spoke. "You didn't tell me you'd had a break-in," he said gently.

I tensed. "I was going to tell you. And it was nothing. They didn't even get in."

"Still, it's important. From what Jimmy tells me, it might have been an inside job, at least partly. I'm going to get background checks on some of the former employees."

I felt stress shoot through my body, just as if someone had injected me with a needle. It seemed like every day had yet more stress these days. "You think we employ criminals?" It came out like an outraged screech, so pathetic I wanted to call the words back in.

"Not currently, no," Damon said, still unruffled by my over-reaction. "Cody checks out, and so does Jimmy here, as soon as he pays his alimony and clears that shit up." He narrowed his gaze on the older man.

"I'm on it, boss," Jimmy said. Then, realizing who he'd spoken to, he turned to me apologetically. "I mean—Sorry, boss."

"It's fine," I said. Somewhere in the back of my brain, I marvelled that Damon could win over someone as street smart as Jimmy so easily. But I didn't really care who Jimmy called boss and who he didn't. I was still stuck on the criminal thing. "You think someone who worked here tried to rob us?" I asked Damon. "Why would they use a baseball bat on the windows instead of just taking money from the till during a shift?"

"Oh, they likely took money from the till," Damon replied. "They also likely blabbed to one too many of their dirtbag friends about how easy it could be to rob the place, which is why someone made a try with a baseball bat. Or, option B, they attempted the robbery after they'd been fired. They could try again, or someone else could. Which is why I'm getting some personnel history." He picked up a pen from my desk—*my* desk

—and spun it effortlessly over the tip of his finger, his gray gaze still unwaveringly on me. "We need to make the Wild safer. We have work to do, Andie."

I felt my cheeks flush. It was the sound of him saying my name that did it. So stupid. "Which is why I asked you for a list." I shot back at him.

Damon seemed to find this amusing. "You're not getting a list. I'm not a list guy. I'm more of an action guy. In the time it takes someone else to write a list, I've already gotten shit done. I'm going to have to spend a little money, though."

"How much money?" I still sounded alarmed. "I'm still going through the books. The Wild doesn't make much profit from what I can see. And Terry left unpaid bills."

"That's because Terry was a shit business owner," Damon said, anger simmering in his voice for the first time. "As well as a shit husband and, apparently, a shit father."

My jaw dropped open in shock.

"Um, should I leave?" Jimmy asked. He was still wide-eyed in his chair, where we'd both forgotten about him.

"What do you know about what kind of husband and father Terry was?" I asked Damon, ignoring Jimmy. I realized we were using *was* as if Terry were dead. It was technically incorrect, but satisfying.

Something flashed across Damon's expression before he tamped it down. "I know enough," he said, his voice tight.

"What does that mean?"

"I gotta go," Jimmy said, getting up from his chair and squeezing past me to leave the office. The door clicked shut behind him.

That was when I knew they had talked about Terry before I'd arrived. "What did he say?" I asked Damon. "What did Jimmy tell you?"

Damon didn't even try to deny it. He ran a hand over his

face, as if the thought of telling me was making him tired. "Don't we have an appointment with one of your suppliers to get to?" he asked.

My jaw clenched. I wanted Damon to answer my question. But—and this wasn't a surprise—I also *didn't* want him to. Whatever it was, was bad; that much, I already knew. I was already dealing with Miles, and this bar, and Terry had already left. Once I signed his stupid addendum, we were divorced. He was with his girlfriend in Florida, and he would never be my problem again. Why did I need even more bad news?

If you don't know about it, it can just go away, a voice in my head said. It was a familiar voice, one I'd been hearing for years now. I never acknowledged it, but I always followed its advice.

If you keep your head down, if you keep your eyes shut and your ears plugged, you can just keep going without being dragged down. Because knowing everything isn't always best, right?

"Yes," I gritted out after a moment of tense silence. "We have an appointment."

There was another moment of silence, just as tense as the first one. Then Damon nodded.

"Okay then," he said. "Let's go."

THIRTEEN

Damon

I WAS FUCKING THIS UP.

I was alienating Andie. I was making her mad. I was overstepping. She was my boss, and I wasn't treating her like it. I wasn't even treating her like an equal. I wasn't treating her like anything at all.

This had always been my problem—well, one of them. Aside from having a lifelong problem with authority—an excellent quality for a federal agent—and a constant instinct to fuck things up just because I could. I also had a hard time with *feelings*. Specifically other people's, and not hurting them. I was bad at it.

I had a talent for saying the wrong thing at the wrong time, even if that thing was true. I had the ability to tell a woman to her face that I wasn't interested in dating her anymore, no excuses, I just wasn't. Or the ability to tell a colleague that I thought he was about to get demoted or laid off. People don't want to hear that stuff. It was something I rarely bothered to remember.

But I didn't want to hurt Andie's feelings. I actually didn't *want* to, which was unusual for me, because usually I just didn't care. And now I had information that I was pretty sure she didn't know, that would hurt her feelings if I gave it to her. And she had asked me to tell her. And I had needed to stop myself, all of which was alien and felt uncomfortable. Everything about Andie made me uncomfortable.

I was here for a job—a free one, at that, at least for now. She was Terry's ex-wife and my boss. I wasn't supposed to sneak glimpses at her ass when she wore those jeans, which she did every day. I wasn't supposed to picture getting her into bed and making her scream. And, worst of all, I wasn't supposed to actually want to help her and somehow protect her feelings.

And yet, I was doing all of it.

I kept my expression distantly professional and my gaze straight ahead as we left the Wild and got into Andie's car. I kept my tone professional as we discussed whether I would drive again, because when I did it gave her time to answer emails and deal with business over her phone. I didn't ask her why she was late this morning or what seemed to have stressed her out so much, because it was none of my business. I got in the driver's seat, got an address from my boss, and started driving.

We were going to a brewery today, a local one that was one of the Wild's top suppliers. Apparently the bar had had Newtown brand beer on tap since the place opened twenty years ago, and it was a favorite of the regulars.

"Our customers say it's really, really good beer," Andie said as she flipped through the papers she'd brought with her in her messenger bag.

"Tragically, I will never know," I replied. "I'll take your word for it."

"Oh, I've never tried it myself. Though maybe I should. With the way today is going, I might start drinking."

I glanced at her as I got on the highway and tapped the gas. "I'm sorry I overstepped back there," I managed. "I shouldn't have used your office without asking you."

It was an apology for the least of my offenses, which was the only apology I could manage. Baby steps.

Andie laughed softly, because she wasn't buying it. "No problem, Damon. Use my office anytime you want."

She didn't deserve this. After spending so many years married to Terry, she deserved to be treated better than I was treating her now. "I'll make your list," I said. "I'll itemize what we need at the Wild to increase security, and I'll get quotes for everything. It's up to you what we do and when."

"How magnanimous of you." She wasn't stupid, this woman. She wasn't going to smile and let me off the hook when I hadn't earned it. Damn it.

I was going to say something else—probably another apology attempt that would be embarrassing in its lameness—when Andie changed the subject.

"Oh, look," she said, her voice dry as she lifted a paper from her small stack. "It seems we owe Newtown Brewing money, too. What a surprise."

"Maybe you won't get hit on this time," I offered.

"Considering we're meeting with a woman, the chances are low."

"But not zero."

Andie put the unpaid bill down and looked at me, her eyebrows going up. "Do you actually think a lesbian would hit on me?"

It seemed to be a serious question, so I answered seriously. "Yes. I do."

Why that made her blush, I had no idea, but her cheeks went red. "That's very flattering, I guess," she said. "Thank you."

I laughed. "I think this is the weirdest conversation I've ever had."

Andie was silent for a moment as I exited the highway and maneuvered through the city streets. "What did Jimmy tell you, Damon?" she asked, her voice soft. "Please tell me. I promise I can take it."

Ah, fuck. I'd let my guard down. I swallowed. "It isn't good," I warned her.

"I promise not to shoot the messenger."

We were almost at the brewery now, and I stalled for time as I signalled to enter the parking lot, then told the security guard who we were here to meet. He waved us to a parking spot in the visitor side of the lot. Andie was still waiting.

"The girlfriend Terry's with now," I said as I parked the car. "He met her at the Wild."

She was silent, digesting that. She hadn't known; I could tell. She nodded slowly. "Okay. Is there more?"

We were sitting in the silent car now, about to go in to a meeting that could be difficult. "Andie—"

"Tell me."

"She wasn't the first." Shit, that hurt to say. Physically hurt, like glass in my throat. I'd never felt that before. "There were women before her that he met at the Wild. Jimmy has only worked there a few months, so he doesn't know when it started. But it's happened at least that long, and likely longer. It's an open secret among the staff."

She flinched at my words—physically flinched, as if something was coming at her. The blush was gone from her cheeks, and now she was pale. When she opened her eyes again, they were empty in a way I didn't like at all.

I had done that to her. Me. Maybe she had asked me for it, but it didn't fucking matter. I had made her look like that, and I felt like shit for it.

"Okay," she said again.

I couldn't think of anything adequate to say. That I was sorry. That I hadn't wanted to tell her, but she forced me to. That it wasn't my fault, or hers. That I could fix it. That I *would* fix it.

I couldn't promise her that. Instead, I said the only true thing that came to my mind. "He's gone, Andie. You're done with him."

"He's still Miles's father." Her voice was a pained croak. "Though you were right about that, too. He's a shit parent. Half the time he doesn't pick up Miles's calls." She shook her head. "So, no, I'm not really done with Terry, am I? I never will be."

"You'll figure out a way to deal with him," I said.

She laughed bitterly. "How do you know that?"

"Because you're smart. You're definitely smarter than Terry. That part isn't even hard."

Andie shook her head at the compliment, such as it was. Then she steeled her spine and put her papers in her messenger bag. "Let's get this meeting over with."

FOURTEEN

Andie

THE OWNER of Newtown Brewing was Ginny Newtown, because it was a family business. Ginny was fortyish, with graying brown hair tied into a high ponytail and dangly, beaded earrings that looked fashionable and awesome. She was brightly dressed in a white blouse and bright orange knee-length skirt. And she wasn't hitting on me, as far as I could tell.

"So you're Terry's ex-wife, huh?" she said as we sat down in her office. She crossed her toned legs and looked me up and down. She was obviously acquainted with Terry, and whatever had happened with him, she wasn't impressed.

I was still raw from what Damon had told me in the parking lot. Terry had been cheating on me for God knew how long, with God knew how many women. I'd suspected it; it was the reason I'd stopped sleeping with my husband. But that didn't make it any easier to hear it confirmed out loud. It seemed that Terry still had the power to make me feel hurt.

Weirdly, the first thing I'd thought was *I'm going to need a blood test done.* Terry and I hadn't had sex in a long time, but who knew what he had given me?

Everything about this was humiliating.

I looked at Ginny, at how attractive she was, and blurted the words: "Please tell me you didn't sleep with him."

She frowned, but it was a look of concern, not of guilt. "Honey, no," she said. Then she turned to Damon, who was sitting in the chair next to me. She looked him up and down, too, a twinkle of interest in her eyes. "Are you the bodyguard?"

"Sort of," he replied.

"Leave the room for a little bit, will you? This is girl talk."

I thought he'd give her attitude, like he usually gave me, but instead something seemed to pass between the two of them. Then Damon shrugged. "Okay," he said, getting up. "I guess I'll go smell vats of beer for a while."

"One of the guys will give you a sample if you want," Ginny said as he walked to the door.

"I'm on the clock," he said, and left.

When the door closed behind him, Ginny looked at me. "What's with that guy?" she asked. "I mean, he's hot. Don't get me wrong. If that's why you bring him everywhere, then I'm all for it. But I get the feeling it's something else."

She said it with such empathy. And I didn't have any women to talk to, because I was an only child and my mother died when I was ten. And everything was too much. To my complete horror, I started to cry.

If Ginny was surprised or embarrassed, she didn't show it. She leaned over, opened a drawer in her desk, and took out a small travel pack of Kleenex, the kind you take with you on a plane. "I always keep these handy," she explained as she passed them to me. "I've had plenty of days when I've cried in this office. I just don't let on."

For some reason that just made me cry harder. I wedged a few Kleenex from the package and mopped my eyes, then blew my nose.

"I'm so sorry," I said to her. "I don't know what came over me."

"No? Well, I do," Ginny said. "You've been married to a complete bastard for a lot of years, that's what. And then he dumped you and you're happy and sad and mad about it all at once. And you have a bar to run. It's a lot."

"It is!" It was so cathartic to hear someone say it out loud. "It really is! I think I'm going crazy."

"Yeah, I get that." Ginny shrugged. "But you didn't answer my question. What's with Hottie Bodyguard? Is he guarding your body or what? Because in my opinion, he should be."

I laughed as I mopped the last of my tears. "I hired him for security. There have been break-ins at the Wild, and some of the crowd there can be rough. Hottie—I mean, Damon is former DEA. He's going to overhaul the bar security for me."

"Fine, so why do you bring him to your meetings?"

For a second, I completely forgot that he'd originally wanted to come to my meetings so he could get a better feel for how the business was run. "It makes me feel better to have him here," I said instead, which I suddenly realized was the truth. "The last guy I met with was a creep who tried to hit on me. No one tries to bother me when Damon is around."

"Yeah, I guess they don't!" Ginny barked a laugh. "He's hot, but he's also scary as shit. It's a good idea, actually. This business is mostly men, and most of those men are horny garbage, especially with a divorced woman who is vulnerable and good-looking. They'll probably see you as fresh meat."

So there was someone else who thought I was attractive, even though she possibly wasn't a lesbian. It was starting to get through my head that Terry was lying all these years when he'd treated me like no sane man would ever look at me. When he'd treated me like I wasn't the least bit sexy or beautiful.

"You think I'm vulnerable?" I asked Ginny.

"Oh, honey. You're practically bleeding all over the floor in here. It's probably why Hottie Bodyguard has such a soft spot for you."

"I don't think he has a soft spot for me," I said, thinking of the conversation we'd had in my office, and then in the car.

"If you say so." Ginny shrugged again, the motion making her earrings move and click. "Maybe you pay him enough to stick around."

"I don't pay him anything. Not yet, anyway. This is kind of a trial thing."

She stared at me, and then she said, "That guy out there," she pointed to the door, "has DEA skills, and he's working for you for free? Are you banging him?"

"No!" My face flushed.

"But you want to. Right? Does he know that?"

"My husband only left two weeks ago." Why was I even having this conversation? Nothing about today was happening like it was supposed to. I dug into my messenger bag and pulled out my trusty papers, trying to get back on track. "I booked this meeting today to talk about your invoices."

Ginny only glanced at the papers I was holding. "It's simple," she said. "Terry didn't pay his bills unless we threatened to sue him. Every time. He's an asshole, I'd bet my grandma's inheritance that he was into something dirty, and yes, he tried to fuck me numerous times. I turned him down. You're well rid of him, honey. You can do a lot better."

"Okay," I said, trying to process all of that. I fixated on one small part of what she'd said. "You think Terry was into something dirty?"

"You get a feeling about some people, you know?" Ginny

said. "I had a feeling about Terry. But I have no proof. Just my gut."

Yeah, well, I'd lived with Terry for years, and it had taken me this long to catch on. Apparently, my gut wasn't as well-honed as Ginny's was.

Or maybe I'd preferred to keep my eyes closed and my ears plugged. Because that was safer.

I didn't want to think about that, about what it meant. If I had kept my head in the sand all of those years, I certainly was paying for it now. "I'm going to make payments on the invoices," I said. "I'm a bookkeeper by trade, so it won't take me long to straighten out the finances. Then we'll start making regular payments on the balance we owe. I'm asking that you don't cut deliveries off in the meantime. I'm going to make it right, I swear. You'll get everything you're owed."

Ginny seemed to think about that, and finally she nodded. "I believe you. We'll keep delivering in good faith for now. Send what you can, when you can, and we'll work it out. Oh, and no cash."

I blinked. "Cash?"

"Yeah. Terry and his cash." She shook her head. "What kind of business does he think I run? This has been my family business for two generations, going on three. I'm not interested in a bag of cash from God knows where to pay my invoices. Just write a check like a normal business. That's all I ask."

"Okay," I said, putting my papers away as a trickle of relief started somewhere in my belly. This was a problem, but I was dealing with it. I could solve it. And I could do it on my own, without help. "I can do that."

"Back to Hottie Bodyguard." Ginny uncrossed her legs and leaned forward. "Let me give you a little advice."

"Advice for what?" I asked.

"How to get him into bed."

I stared at her, my mind blank of words.

"That's what you want, right?" She waved a hand. "Of course it is. All those years with Terry? You need to get laid by someone proper. That man is proper." She pointed at the door again. "It won't be easy, though. Men like that never are. When they're tough to crack, they're usually dynamite in bed. Totally worth it." She nodded, as if this was a two-way conversation, when in fact I was so embarrassed I could barely breathe. "My suggestion is to start a bit of a fight with him. Nothing too serious, you know, just a spat. Get him going. Provoke him, make him a little bit mad. It will make the sex that much hotter. And the make-up sex?" She whistled. "Lord, you'll need a fire extinguisher."

"I don't want fire extinguisher sex," I managed to croak.

"Sure you do, honey. We all do, it's just that not all of us get the opportunity. If you can't get him to fight with you, find some other way to get his blood up. Challenge him to something physical." She snapped her fingers as she got an idea. "I know. Ask him to give you self-defense lessons. Then he has to put his hands on you, try to pin you to the ground. Oh, that's good. He'll bang you for sure. Maybe right there on the floor."

"Stop," I said. I was tempted to put my hands over my ears, like Miles used to do when he was a toddler and he didn't want to hear me tell him to go to bed. "He doesn't—You have the wrong idea. Damon isn't interested in me like that. We've only known each other for a few days."

Ginny smiled. "A few days is long enough for a man to decide he wants to fuck you. A few *minutes* is long enough."

"I know, but I'm not his type." I couldn't believe I was talking about this. "I'm not confident and sexy like you are. I mean, maybe I could be those things, but not yet. Right now I'm a mom, I'm a mess, I'm almost divorced, and I'm close to broke. I've been married for a million years to a man who didn't appreciate me, and I have no idea how to seduce someone, let alone Damon. I don't even own any sexy underwear. You're teaching the Ph.D., and I'm still in the 101 class."

"Okay." Ginny tapped her nails on the desk. "Just think about it, okay? Because if I know anything about men, then he's thinking about it already."

I WAS COMPOSED by the time I came out of Ginny's office, where Damon was waiting in the hallway, leaning against the wall and scrolling on his phone. He looked up at me, raising his brows. "Everything go okay?"

"Yes." I walked past him, heading down the hall toward the exit. I tried not to let on that I currently had a mental image of him banging me on the floor. "Let's go."

His hand touched my arm, and I stopped. Damon had never touched me before; we hadn't even shaken hands when we made our agreement. It was as if he had decided I had a bubble around me that he wouldn't break. Maybe that bubble was named Terry. Or maybe it was just me.

But he was touching me now, and even through the sleeve of my blouse, I felt the heat of it on my skin. Although his grip was gentle, I couldn't have kept walking if my life depended on it.

"Andie, look at me," he said.

I forced myself to turn. His gray eyes were fixed on me, their expression serious. He was so close that I caught his scent.

"I'm sorry about earlier," he said. "I'm sorry I had to tell you that stuff."

I let out a soft breath, still unable to move. "It's okay. I asked."

"You did, but I'm still sorry. Are you going to be all right?"

The usual responses rose to my lips. *Of course. I'm fine. I'm just fine.* But I found that I couldn't say them, considering I'd sobbed in Ginny's office not thirty minutes ago.

"I'll get through," I said. "I suspected it, to be honest. Still, it wasn't fun to hear. I think... I think I need a little help."

Damon's eyes never left mine. "I'm not going anywhere," he said, his voice soft.

I nodded.

He pulled away, his expression slowly closing down. The moment was over. He dropped his hand from my arm, and we started walking toward the exit again.

I could still feel the heat of his hand on me. Now I was *really* picturing him banging me on the floor. I reminded myself that it was completely inappropriate, and I cleared my throat. "We owe Newtown a lot of money," I said, changing the subject, "but Ginny and I worked out terms. She's going to keep delivering if I start making payments."

"That's good," Damon said as we walked into the parking lot. The soft sincerity was gone from his voice, as if I'd imagined it, and his tone was all business. "I wandered around while you were in there, and this place gets the thumbs up from me. It seems like a legit family business." We stopped next to my car and he patted his pockets, then ran a hand through his hair, tension in every line of his body.

"What's the matter?" I asked, putting my sunglasses on so I could look at him while he couldn't read my expression. He was wearing jeans and a black tee with his leather coat. A perfectly normal outfit for a man to wear, but lordy. Since that frank conversation with Ginny, I could admit that I really liked looking at him.

He blew out a breath, then took my car keys from his pocket. "I really want a cigarette," he admitted. "No big deal."

I stared at him in shock. "You mean you actually did it? You quit smoking because I told you to?"

I knew the answer already, I realized. If Damon had been smoking, I would be able to smell it, especially when we were so close together in the car. But he didn't smell like cigarettes today, just like clean laundry and some kind of pheromone that apparently turned me into a woman who called him Hottie Bodyguard behind his back.

He shrugged in answer to my question. "It was time to do it," he said. "You were right. I already gave up drinking and drugs, and then I survived getting shot twice. It seems pretty stupid to kill myself after all that." He smiled and ran another hand through his dark blond hair, mussing it a little. "I put one of those patches on. See?" He shrugged off one shoulder of his coat and pulled up the sleeve of his black tee, showing me the patch on his shoulder.

"Um," I said, because I was temporarily transfixed by the smooth, taut skin of his biceps and the ink on it. "Is that an octopus?"

"Yeah." Damon angled his arm so I could see it better. Sure enough, he had a tattoo of an octopus on his biceps, the tentacles waving across his skin. "You like it?"

"I do. Are you a diver?"

"Not even close. I was drunk that night and I don't even remember getting it. Luckily, I think it's cool. It could have been a lot worse." He pulled his sleeve back down and shrugged his jacket back on, and inside I drooped with disappointment. "Anyway, I'm definitely off the cigarettes. It's making me crazy though, even with the patch. And if my smokes are still in your purse, it's possible I'll steal them off you, so please throw them out."

"What?" It took me a second to remember that when I'd so

rudely told Damon to quit smoking, I'd put his cigarettes in my purse. I hadn't taken them out, but—

Wait a minute.

I opened my purse and looked inside. Nope, there were definitely no cigarettes in there. I hadn't taken them out, and neither had Damon.

It couldn't be. Could it?

"What?" Damon asked, looking at my stricken expression.

"Shit," I said. "I think my son stole your cigarettes."

FIFTEEN

Damon

BY THE END of my second week working for Andie and the Wild, we had settled into a kind of routine. By day, she'd work in the office, cleaning up the books and the finances while I came and went from the bar, upgrading security. I'd given her the list she'd asked for, and we started working through the items on it based on how urgent they were and how much they cost. The first thing we tackled was installing a security system, including coded door entry, cameras outside the front door, and cameras behind the bar. So I dealt with buying and installing the system while Andie worked at her desk.

At four every day, I sent Andie home to her son, while she argued guiltily that I worked too many hours for no pay. Then, as the evening crowds came in, I took over the office, upgrading the computer and file security. Thursday, Friday, and Saturday I'd stay late to bounce drunks, of which there were a good number. The other nights I'd go home at eight, after checking with Jimmy that he could handle things alone.

That was most days except Sunday, which was Andie's day off. And on the days when she had supplier meetings, I'd drive her.

I didn't mind the long hours. I didn't have much to do at home except watch TV while Carl's music seeped up through the floor. Spring was advancing in Colorado, and I took up jogging, going for longer and longer runs during the cool evenings as my endurance improved. I'd been fit when I worked for the DEA, pushing my body regularly in strength training, but since the shooting I hadn't been able to work out. Adding cigarettes to the mix meant I could do even less. But there must be something to the idea of the Rocky Mountain high, because the more time I spent in Salt Springs, the more I felt my strength coming back. I was even eating again.

It still wasn't easy. No matter how bad they were for me, I craved cigarettes all the fucking time, because addiction is like that. I was well acquainted with it. My first day off from the Wild I found a local AA meeting in Salt Springs, held in a church basement, and I started going regularly. I hadn't had a drink in seven years, but that didn't matter. AA meetings are something you do for life, whenever you need it, no explanation necessary. The meetings helped me with the cigarette cravings, kept me honest, kept me from backsliding into the other, worse stuff. So I went.

I barely recognized this version of myself. The DEA job had been my identity for so long that I wasn't sure where Damon Blake, bar security guy, had come from. He wasn't the bitter asshole I'd been as a young man, but he wasn't much to write home about, either. At least he was eating a sandwich every once in a while and getting a few hours of sleep at night. That was the best I could do.

My downstairs neighbor, Carl, wasn't quite buying the new me. He gave me suspicious looks anytime we passed each other on the front driveway, and he was practically hostile the one time I saw him lifting his heavy garbage can to the curb and helped him with it.

"You're awfully quiet," he said when I heaved the can into place.

"I thought that's what you wanted." I was only a little bit out of breath. Fuck, that can was heavy. What was an old guy throwing out that weighed that much? Did he have a body in there?

"I'll admit you don't stomp on the floor," Carl said as I brushed my palms off on my jeans. "You don't do much else, either."

"I work a lot," I said.

"Huh. You have a girl?"

I immediately thought of Andie, who was definitely not my girl. "No."

He peered at me closely, because he was far from stupid. "But there's a girl you like?"

"Maybe." What the hell was I doing? Was I having a conversation with my eighty-year-old neighbor that belonged in eighth grade? Jesus, Andie wasn't even a girl, she was a thirty-five-year-old woman. Next Carl would tell me to pass her notes in class.

I almost liked the guy, but then he ruined it by saying, "Well, I'm glad you like *some* girl. I was starting to wonder if you were a gay."

I looked him dead in the eyes long enough that he started to fidget. Just gave him that cold, soulless look that I'd used to break so many suspects in the interview room. He was practically sweating when I finally leaned forward and gave him a clap on the shoulder.

"I'm not a gay," I said, my voice flat. "But thanks for asking."

He stayed out of my business after that. I felt like we'd reached an understanding.

I used that same dead-eyed look on any guy at the Wild who looked at Andie too long or let his gaze drop to her ass. I used it on the sales rep from a huge beer company who was definitely working up to hitting on her while they talked delivery schedules. I had mastered that look. It was effective every time.

My problem was that yes, I liked Andie, just as if I was in eighth grade. She was sexy and smart and she was raising a kid and putting her back into the business, determined to make it pay the bills. I wanted to get her into bed so bad my body ached with it. I wanted to do all kinds of things to her that maybe she'd never even imagined.

She was also the ex, or near-ex, of my former colleague. Not that I felt I owed any loyalty to Terry. I just had a bad track record with married women.

I hadn't told Andie that part of my life.

Boner for my boss or not, I still had the gut feeling that there was something wrong with this setup of Terry's, so I had put feelers out. The Salt Springs PD had pretty much told me to go fuck myself when I called and identified myself, asking for information on a few of the Wild's former employees. Local police and the Feds have a hate-hate relationship, and my DEA credentials meant the local guys wouldn't talk to me.

I had reached out to a few former Fed colleagues, looking to get some information though back routes, but they were giving me the polite runaround. No one wanted to risk his job or his next promotion by helping me with a case that wasn't even a case, just a hunch. They sure as hell didn't want anything to do with a situation that could involve Terry. The whole thing was kryptonite, and no one wanted to touch it.

That left me stuck. I was used to being the guy who had access to all the information he needed, even the stuff no one wanted me to know. Being locked out was unfamiliar to me. I had put a call in to a local PI, which meant I'd have to pay his bill out of my own pocket, because there was no way Andie would agree to snoop on people who didn't even work for her anymore. But my gut wouldn't let me drop it, and I'd trusted my gut for my entire career. It hadn't led me wrong, except maybe for the time I'd been in the wrong place at the wrong time during a major bust and gotten myself shot.

Okay, maybe that one time. But this was different.

I hadn't gotten an email back from the private investigator. What I did have in my inbox was an email from my brother, Alex. He and his wife, Kat, had just gotten married in Italy. It was the second time they got married, after marrying a long time ago and divorcing. It's possible I had something to do with that.

Alex also had a prison record, and it was possible I had something to do with that, too.

He and Kat were reunited now, all these years later, and they were happy, but it didn't change the fact that I had done some very bad things in my life. Things that people with feelings didn't do. Things that people who love other people, who love their family, don't ever do.

Alex and Kat had invited me to their wedding. I hadn't gone. Maybe they could forgive me, but it didn't change the fact that I couldn't forgive myself. I wasn't a good bet. Not for anyone. I hadn't even sent them a wedding gift. It was better this way.

I read over Alex's brief email. I could see that he had

attached photos to it, pictures of his wedding to his beautiful wife. I didn't open the photos.

I didn't delete the email, either.

Instead, I closed my laptop and went for another run.

SIXTEEN

Andie

THE STOREROOM at the Wild was in a back corner, down the hall from the office, in an awkward, cramped space with a single overhead light. We kept cases of booze in there, as well as other bar-type things like napkins, straws, cleaning supplies, and fresh lemons and limes. The Wild didn't serve food of any kind—even those damned annoying peanuts that some bars give out so people can make an unholy mess with the shells. The building didn't even have a kitchen. It was a bar where you went for just one purpose: to get drunk. I had to admit, it made the business easier to run.

I had figured out where we ordered napkins from, and I didn't know if we needed more. I got up from my desk and walked down the hall to the storeroom, my keys in my hand. The door was already open, the single light inside turned on. I peeked in to see Damon in there.

He was standing in the middle of the room, his head tilted

back as he looked up at a top shelf. There was a brief second before he noticed me, and I took him in. In the three weeks since he'd first come through the door of the Wild, he had changed in subtle ways. He wasn't as painfully thin, and his body was solid and vital. He was less pale, his cheekbones less drawn. He'd had a barber trim his beard close to his jawline, and he'd had a haircut too, though he still wore it just long enough for the bad-boy look. He wasn't wearing his jacket, and I could see the octopus tattoo on his biceps beneath the sleeve of his tee.

I felt a mix of things when I looked at him: lust, uncertainty, tentative liking that grew stronger every day, fear, more lust. Did I mention lust?

I wasn't used to being hot for a man—not just distantly admiring, but *hot*. And I was hot for Damon Blake. The fact that I could admit that to myself at all meant that something was changing in me—something I didn't understand, but was starting to like. A lot. It was fun to be in lust with a hot guy I worked with, fun to have an excuse to spend time with him every day, fun to take him on appointments with me so he could be his scary self. I hadn't allowed myself to have fun since —well, I could barely remember the last time I'd had fun. This was a quiet kind of fun that I got to enjoy without hurting anyone.

I wasn't sure how he felt about me. Damon didn't seem to mind spending time with me, but he was hard to read. Since those first few times we'd argued, he'd seemed to be careful with me. He didn't start any more fights. He also didn't make a move.

Did I want him to? Part of me—the newer, sexier part—did want him to, but the thought was also terrifying. If Damon actually tried anything with me, I'd probably freeze up in a silent freakout. That was the reality, not the fantasy.

I cleared my throat. "Hey," I said.

Damon turned, looking at me. "Oh. Hey."

I stepped into the storeroom. "What's so fascinating in here?"

"I was looking for a spot to put the security sensor."

I followed his gaze upward to where the wall met the ceiling. "I thought we were putting in cameras?"

Damon shook his head. "The wireless signal doesn't work in here, so cameras are out unless we re-wire the entire hallway. But a simple sensor will track when the door opens and closes. It's easier to do. That isn't what I was looking at, though." He pointed to the top shelf. "There's a crate of Sheffer whiskey up there."

I followed where he was pointing. "Okay."

"There's another crate of the same thing behind it. And there are three bottles of Sheffer behind the bar right now."

I frowned. That was a lot of whiskey. After three weeks, I knew how much we went through on average. I stood closer to Damon, peering up. "I didn't order any extra." I hadn't talked to Dave, the creep from Sheffer Whiskey, since our meeting three weeks ago. I wasn't eager to talk to him. I also hadn't sent him any money on our owed invoices yet, so it was odd that we somehow had more supply that we hadn't paid for.

"I figured you didn't. I'll ask the staff if they know where this came from and when. Once we have the sensors in here, we'll know who has been in and out."

"Okay," I said. "If Dave thinks he's getting paid anytime soon for that extra case, he's dreaming. It'll take us two months to get through all of that."

Damon looked at me. "Was there something you came in here for?"

Oh. Right. "I figured out the ordering system for our napkin supplier. Do we need any?"

We spent fifteen minutes searching the shelves for cocktail napkins, only to find that we were almost out. I had figured out how to order more just in time. "I can't believe Terry ran this business even for a day," Damon grumbled. "He sucks at being an entrepreneur."

"Well, it isn't his business anymore," I replied, re-shelving the last package of napkins. "It's mine."

"I thought it was already yours," he said. "You're the only one running it."

"It's mine on paper, though. Officially." I felt a flush of accomplishment, mixed with a weird combination of terror and shame, as I said the next words. "My divorce from Terry is final. The papers are all signed. He signed this place over to me, so it's officially mine now. He has no claim on it anymore."

Damon's gaze rested on me for a long moment, and I couldn't read his expression. "Congratulations," he said, his voice low.

"Thanks." My cheeks flushed hot, like they sometimes did around him. "This means I'm a new woman, right?"

"Sure." He smiled a little. "I'd say we celebrate with a drink, but neither of us drink. At least, not anything good."

I nodded. "Right, yes. I mean, no. We don't drink."

His gaze hadn't moved from me, and it was making my blood rush hotter. "You know why I don't drink," he said. "But you never told me why you don't."

"I just don't like it." It was true. Terry and I had been tipsy the night I'd conceived Miles, and then when I was pregnant, I couldn't drink. After that, I found I just didn't like to lose control the way you could when you were drunk. My life was already out of control enough. I wanted to feel like I was doing my best to steer the ship.

I still had no desire to drink, even though I was now the official owner of a bar. But I was changing in other ways. Maybe, just this once, I could take a risk.

I thought about Ginny's advice, and for once, I decided to go for it.

"Can I ask you something?" I said to Damon.

"Sure."

I braced myself. What would Ginny do in this situation, alone in the storeroom with Hottie Bodyguard? I didn't feel like starting a fight with him, so I decided on option two.

"Would you, um..." I forced the words out. "Would you teach me self defense?"

There was a moment of silence, and then Damon frowned, confused. "You want to learn self defense?"

"Yes. You know, a few moves. Just in case." I wouldn't let myself sound lame. I'd sound confident instead. I held my chin up. "I'd like to know how to defend myself."

He seemed to think it over, and then he nodded. My heart sped up. "Sure," he said. "I can teach you self defense."

Was this actually working? "Thanks. Do you want to do it here or—"

"Here's your self defense lesson, Andie," Damon said before I could spit out the rest. "Run."

I stared at him, confused. "What?"

He shook his head. "The best method of self defense is always to get yourself out of the situation. Don't engage. The other person could be stronger than you, or could be mentally unbalanced, or could be armed. He could be on something. There's nothing I hate more than the way self defense classes market themselves as a way to fight off an attacker. As a cop, I'm giving you the advice that is most likely to actually save your life. If anything happens, escape any way you possibly can." He nodded at my stunned expression, oblivious to the fact that he'd just lectured his way out of my making a pass at him. "I'm gonna go shop for sensors. I'll see you later."

I WAS in my office ten minutes later when my phone rang. It was my dad.

"What the hell is wrong with that guy you hired?" he said when I answered.

"I don't know." I bit the words out. I was embarrassed and frustrated and still a little bit horny. "He's a jerk." An oblivious one. Jesus, how stupid could one man be?

"He's nosy is what he is," my dad said. "I got a call from one of my old colleagues. Your new guy, this DEA guy I looked up —he's been trying to do some background checks of his own. On your other employees."

"I know." Damon had already told me he was going to try this. "What does he want?"

"He's asking questions about some of Terry's employees, the ones that don't work there anymore. Some other stuff, too. The Salt Springs PD told him to go pound sand, since he isn't law enforcement anymore. But something tells me he'll find another way to get the information he wants. I thought you hired him to bounce drunks and put in a security system."

"He's doing those things, too," I said, defensive.

"Yeah, well, he isn't making any friends in this town. Keep an eye on him, Andie. You don't have a business brain, and you don't know much about hiring people. He could be up to something and you wouldn't know. He could outsmart you."

"Gee, thanks, Dad." I had no idea why his comments still stung. I'd been hearing them all my life. *He means well.* That was always the excuse with my dad, the reason to keep putting up with him. *He means well. And he doesn't talk to Miles like this.*

When he was with Miles, my impossible-to-please father became a fawning grandfather, convinced his grandson was destined to be the greatest at everything he tried. *Have you seen him play soccer? What a kick he has. Low marks on a math test? There's something wrong with that teacher.* With Terry's complete failure as a father, Miles needed all of the unconditional love he could get. So I put up with Dad, I never fought with him, and I let him see Miles as often as he wanted.

Miles and I had been on shaky ground for weeks now. I'd reamed him about stealing the cigarettes from my purse, which he'd at first denied and then admitted. Then I'd had to deal with the fact that his marks were sinking. There had been meetings with teachers, sulky refusals to eat dinners, and slammed bedroom doors—his, not mine. I was still the adult in this situation, at least for now.

We had an uneasy truce, but he didn't trust me. He didn't seek me out or tell me anything. My father thought I was stupid and my son thought I was evil, but the two of *them* got along just fine. It was me that no one gave a shit about anymore.

"Damon is not up to something," I said to my dad. "He's doing his job. And he's a big help around here."

"Maybe you should call Terry and ask what he thinks."

Was he kidding? "You hate Terry!" I said, sounding like a crazy woman for the first time in this conversation.

"Hate is a strong word," Dad said, as if I hadn't had to listen to his opinion of Terry for thirteen years. "He knows this Blake guy, and he used to run the Wild. He might know what you should do."

Of course. Even the dirtbag my father despised, who had left me for his girlfriend, must be better at this than me. "I am not asking Terry," I snapped. Terry had already told me to fire

Damon, which made me more determined than ever to keep Damon employed. "Terry is gone. We're officially divorced, and the bar is officially mine. He has nothing to do with this."

"Jesus, you're so touchy," my father complained. "I'm just making a suggestion. I'm just trying to help. You don't even appreciate it."

I thought of Miles. I thought of how much he loved his grandfather and how much he needed him right now. "I have to go," I gritted out, though the words made my jaw hurt.

I hung up feeling more tired and more raw than I could remember feeling, even the day Terry left. I was sick of men. I was like a battery that has been drained dry, emptied of everything while I gave and gave to other people. I wanted someone to bring me a hot meal and give me a shoulder rub. And then give me an orgasm, especially if that person was Damon. But right now, that possibility was so remote there was no point even picturing it.

I was a mother, a daughter, an ex-wife, and a business owner. That was all. Apparently I was so out of practice being an actual woman that men didn't even notice when I was trying to seduce them.

Yeah. This was going really, really well.

SEVENTEEN

Damon

"IT ISN'T WORKING," Andie said.

"Yes, it is," I said. "You have to click the menu on the side. Right there."

Andie leaned in, staring at the screen. We were sitting together in her office, where I had pulled up a chair to sit next to her behind the desk. I was teaching her how to log in to the new security system to track the entry codes to the front and back doors and pull up footage from the cameras if she wanted it. We were doing this on the new computer I'd made her splurge for, one that had an updated operating system that was harder to hack and worked much better than the old one that had been bought God knew when. And yes, the new computer had a password on it.

There was a learning curve, and Andie needed me to walk her through it. So now I was sitting as close to her as I'd ever been, close enough to see the clip she'd twisted into her dark curly hair to tie it off her neck. Close enough to smell whatever she'd put on her skin, something that smelled sweet and vaguely sexy. Close enough that if I dropped my gaze, I might see a few inches down her shirt into her cleavage. I did not drop my gaze.

Instead, I leaned past her and pointed to two different menu buttons. "This one gives you the live video feed. This one gives you the recorded feed that you can search through if you need it."

I thought I heard her take a breath as I got close. I paused, feeling the silent electricity between us spark. I always got this feeling when I was with Andie, like my skin was suddenly over-sensitive. It was an amazing feeling, and it was torture at the same time. Because I couldn't do anything about it.

Make no mistake: I wanted to have sex with Andie English. I'd wanted it from the first day, and I wanted it now more than ever. I wanted to watch her skin flush. I wanted to feel the heated skin of her inner thighs. I wanted to taste her. I wanted to feel her nails on my back and her breath on my skin as I made her come.

I wanted Andie like I'd never wanted any other woman. But Andie was different, and the situation, to put it mildly, was fucking complicated. I was her employee, originally hired by her hated ex-husband. Her personal life was a mess, and she was still bruised from being cheated on, dumped, and divorced. She was trying to be a single mother. The last thing she needed was a guy like me, a drifter with no purpose in life and a metric ton of problems, trying to get into her pants.

If I put my mind to it, I might be able to seduce her. I might have shit personal skills—and it might have been literally years since I'd actually dated someone—but even I knew that if I really tried, if I paid Andie compliments and asked her out on dates, it was possible I could persuade her to go to bed with me.

But then what? We work together, feeling awkward, until my time at the Wild was up and I left town again?

I'd end up being that mistake she'd made when she was newly divorced and vulnerable. The rebound lay. The mistake she regretted and would never make again. Just like I was the mistake for most of the women I'd dated.

I didn't want to be her mistake. It didn't matter that I had started to get vibes from Andie, signals that maybe she didn't hate me as much as she had the first day I showed up. Signals that she was starting to think about me the way I thought about her. Being a mistake wasn't good enough for me anymore, especially when it came to Andie.

I wasn't entirely sure what I wanted from Andie. But whatever it was, I was pretty sure it was too soon for her to give it to me.

My time was almost up. We'd agreed that I'd work for her for four weeks, and that was over in a few days. I didn't want to leave, but I also knew that although Andie was getting things under control, the Wild wasn't making a ton of money. I should probably earn something at some point. And if I kept working for Andie for free, it would *really* look like I wanted to sleep with her.

I wasn't going to think about that right now. I had her sitting next to me right here, right now. I'd focus on that instead.

She clicked on the button for the current security feed, and a window opened, showing the view from the camera mounted above the front door. A car passed by in the frame, and two people walked by on the sidewalk, chatting.

"Oh, wow!" Andie said, as if she'd opened a Christmas present. "This is so cool!"

"Click the arrow at the bottom," I told her.

She did, and the picture changed to a live feed from the camera mounted above the bar. We'd positioned this one carefully, so the frame included the cash and part of the bar itself. Andie was adamant that she didn't want her employees to be on camera at all times. But if anyone took from the till, we'd be able to see it. And we also had a good shot of the customers in case anyone got into an argument and we needed to check the record.

We didn't have a camera in the storeroom, but I walked Andie through the options to check the records from the sensors, recording when the door was opened and what code was used. There was a different code for management and employees.

"This is amazing," Andie said as she looked through it. "Everything you've done is amazing."

Why did that make me feel good? It was just a simple thing, getting a few cameras and a feed installed. I tried to remember what normal people said in situations like this, instead of cold silence. "You're welcome," I managed. "If you want to look at the list I gave you, we can move on to the next thing. This office needs more security."

Andie paused and I heard her breath hitch again. When she spoke, her voice was soft. "We're running out of time."

So she was going to bring it up. I couldn't talk about leaving while I was this close to her, so I reluctantly pushed my chair back, out of her space, giving her room to turn and face me.

"Yeah," I said. "I guess we are."

Andie turned. She was wearing a tank top beneath a thin gray hoodie, and I had no idea why it was so sexy, but it was. I could see the dip of skin above the neckline of the tank top, which was only partway zipped. I could see the perfect, elegant line of her neck, and the tiny silver earrings in her ears. She was blushing. Fuck me, she was blushing.

"We should discuss what's going to happen," she said. "With us."

She meant our business relationship, but it sounded like more. For just a split second, I let it be more. I let my gaze move over her flawless throat again, and the words came out of my mouth, unthinking. "I'm not leaving."

Her eyebrows went up in surprise.

"I mean, not if you don't want me to," I amended. "I don't want to leave."

"Oh." She looked flustered. She trained her gaze anywhere but at me. "Well, I—Um, yes. I think—" She looked at the time on her phone. "Damn it, Miles will be home any minute."

It was four o'clock, the time I usually sent her home. "Go ahead," I said. "Things are quiet here. It'll be fine."

She let out a breath. "Damon."

"Andie."

Our eyes met, and she blushed again, shaking her head at the absurdity of her own reaction. "Would you like to come over for dinner?" she asked in a rush. "To discuss things. With both Miles and me, of course."

No way was she asking me on an actual date. We couldn't get into much trouble with her thirteen-year-old son sitting there, as much as both of us might want to. "Sure, I'll come."

"You will?" She seemed pleased, as if she'd expected me to refuse. "How about six o'clock? I'll go home now and start something."

"Don't go to any trouble. I don't eat much. How about I bring takeout and you don't have to do anything at all?"

"No way. I'm cooking. I'm a good cook, and Miles doesn't appreciate it. Besides, when was the last time anyone cooked for you?"

I frowned. "I can't remember the last time. Maybe never."

"Then I'm doing it." Andie pushed her chair back, gathering her purse. "Is spaghetti and meatballs okay?"

"It's fine."

"Okay, then." She smiled. "See you at six."

SHE TEXTED ME HER ADDRESS, and I tried hard to believe it. She was going to cook for me. Andie English was going to cook for me, at her house, and we were going to talk. Sure, Miles would be there, but that was fine with me. It made everything on the up and up, instead of me trying to get my boss into bed. We were going to eat spaghetti and meatballs and talk business.

It sounded normal. It sounded...good.

I should have known it wasn't going to happen.

I got into my car at a quarter to six. I had the key in my hand, ready to put it in the ignition, when my phone rang. It was Andie.

My stomach sank. No way was she calling me for something good. Not now.

I picked up. "Hey, Andie."

"Damon." There was a pause, and I felt the heat of rejection wash over me, the kind of pain I'd never thought I'd feel again. The last time I'd felt rejection like this, I'd been in my twenties and Kat Sloane, the woman who was in love with my brother, had told me she'd never be interested in me. And she never was.

"It's okay," I managed to say.

"It isn't okay." Her voice cracked, and for the first time it crossed my mind that maybe she didn't call just to stomp all over my hopes. "I didn't—I didn't know who else to call."

There was definitely something wrong. I sat up straighter in my seat. "What's going on?"

"I don't know," Andie said. "Miles hasn't come home. And he isn't answering his phone."

EIGHTEEN

Andie

THERE WERE two voices in my head. The first one said: *It's only been a few hours. He's thirteen. He could be with a friend somewhere, and he either dropped his phone or the battery is dead. He's just being a thoughtless teenager. He's fine.* The other voice said: *Call the police.*

If I called the police, the next call the cops made would be to my dad. Did I want to panic my dad? Miles was always home by five, and it was almost six. I could understand if he was just late, but Miles never—*never*—left me hanging without answering my calls or texts, or without letting me know where he was. My calls were now going directly to voicemail, as if his phone was off. Every cell of my body screamed that something was wrong, yet he was only late by an hour. I was a mess.

Instead of calling the police, I did the next best thing. I called Damon.

He showed up at my door in ten minutes. "Tell me every-thing," he said.

I turned off the pots that were simmering on the stove, the spaghetti and meatballs we weren't going to eat, and I let all the words out. About my agreement with Miles taking his bike instead of the school bus, about his five o'clock curfew, about his phone. I babbled that maybe I was overreacting and maybe I was crazy, but this just wasn't like him. I tried Miles's phone again and again, listening it going to voicemail each time.

Everything was going through my head. Miles in a ditch with a head injury after falling off his bike. Miles abducted by a creep. Miles getting hit by a car and admitted to a hospital somewhere, lying in a bed while no one knew who he was. Miles stranded in the middle of nowhere, his bike broken, forced to walk or hitchhike to get home.

I had already called the small hospital in Salt Springs, who didn't have any unidentified boys admitted. What if he'd somehow ended up at a hospital in Denver? What if he wasn't in a hospital at all, but was lying somewhere, hurt?

Damon listened as I talked. When I finally paused to take a breath, he put a hand on the back of my neck. His touch was warm and strong, assured, and I went still, feeling the heat from the contact spread over my skin. I took my first deep breath in a long time. Even the scent of him calmed me down a little. I closed my eyes and breathed in again.

"We'll figure it out," Damon said, his voice calm.

"Okay," I said, my eyes still closed.

He dropped his hand, and I wanted to protest. I needed him touching me. I couldn't make myself say it.

"When was the last time you heard from Miles?" Damon asked me.

Opening my eyes, I pulled out my phone, scrolling back

through my texts. "I haven't heard from him since he left for school this morning. If he hadn't showed up at school, they would have called me, so he must have gone. He usually texts me after school when he's on his way home."

"Okay." Damon was standing close to me as I scrolled through my phone, looking for a text that wasn't there. "We can —Wait. What is that?"

I had closed my text screen, showing the wallpaper on my phone. It was a photo of Miles and me, taken on a hike we'd done a few months ago, both of us tousled and smiling with backpacks on. "What do you mean?" I asked Damon. "That's Miles and me."

He took my phone from my hand and looked closely at the photo. His expression went hard. "Oh, shit."

"What? Oh shit what? Just say it, Damon. You're freaking me out."

He cleared his throat. "I've seen this kid before."

"What? When? Today?"

"Not today." He looked at the photo again, then handed the phone back to me. "I've seen him around town twice now. I didn't know he was your son."

"Around town? What does that mean? Miles goes to school and back. Where would you see him?"

"I saw him at a gas station the first day I came to town."

I was so rattled that his words didn't compute. "That was a month ago. A gas station? Why would Miles be at a gas station?"

Damon tilted my chin up so I was looking into his eyes. His gaze was hard and determined. "Andie," he said. "Take a deep breath. Right now."

"But—"

"Do it."

I inhaled.

"You're not going to panic," Damon said. "You're not going to judge. You're just going to listen while I explain, because you're a rational woman and we're going to get to the bottom of this. Okay?"

I let out a breath and nodded. And then Damon told me.

Miles had been at a gas station, shoplifting snacks. He'd run from the store clerk and gotten into a car that drove away.

Miles had been outside a liquor store with another boy, the two of them waiting for someone inside to come out. He'd gotten into a car that time, too, and it drove away. Damon and I cross-checked the dates. That was the evening Miles told me he was at his friend Jonathan's.

Damon's voice was calm, keeping me from spiralling. "What's Jonathan's phone number?" he asked me.

I shook my head. "I don't know. I always contact Miles on his own phone."

"What's Jonathan's last name?"

Shit. "I don't know—Wait. I had Miles text me Jonathan's address that night." I scrolled through my texts again, going back a few weeks. "Here it is."

"Fine. We'll go there right now."

"I can't," I said. "I can't leave. What if Miles comes home?"

He nodded. "Okay then, I'll go. I'll knock on their door and let you know what happens."

He turned to leave, but I grabbed his arm. "Thank you," I said.

He just nodded again. "You'll hear from me in a few minutes."

He left, and I sat alone in the silent house. I turned up the volume on my phone to the highest possible setting and placed it on the kitchen counter where I could clearly see it. Then, to keep my hands busy, I cleaned up the dinner I'd been making, putting it away in the fridge because when Miles came home, he'd probably be hungry. I was going to think positive if I could.

Thirty minutes that felt like a year later, the phone on the counter rang. It was Damon.

"There's a kid named Jonathan Traeger who lives here," he told me when I answered. "He's two years older than Miles. His parents say Miles has been over a few times and they know who he is. But he wasn't there today, and Jonathan is out." He paused. "They admit that Jonathan has been getting into trouble lately, mostly with his older brother, Jaden. They have no idea where either boy is right now."

I wanted to scream: *Why don't those people know where their children are?* But I couldn't really say that, could I? I didn't know where my own son was.

"Damon, what do I do?" I asked. "Should I call my father?"

"Why would you call your father?"

Of course—I'd never told Damon about my dad. "He was a county sheriff until he retired a few years ago."

There was a beat of silence as Damon digested this. "Does he still have connections with his old colleagues?"

Despite my panic, I snorted a laugh. "Of course he does. He plays poker with half the sheriff's office and the Salt Springs PD on Friday nights. I haven't called the police about Miles because Dad will hear about this within seconds."

"And what will he do?" Damon asked.

"Yell at me," I answered honestly. "Spend too much time lecturing me about how this is my fault as a parent instead of coming up with solutions. Bring it up to my dying day. He adores Miles."

"You'll have to put up with it," Damon said. "I have the license plate of the car I saw Miles get into at the liquor store. We need him to get someone to run it."

"You have the license plate number?"

"It was a gut feeling," Damon said. "You get those when you're a cop for a long time. I'll text you the number. I'll bet anything that car is registered to this Jaden Traeger kid. Chances are, he's with Miles right now. Then we'll find them."

NINETEEN

Damon

IN MY YEARS with the DEA, I had worked on cases involving some of the most terrifying drug importers and dealers you can imagine. Guys who had no souls, whose underlings regularly disappeared, never to be found again. Guys whose girlfriends and wives ended up in the hospital over and over again, or dead. Guys it took us years, and dozens of agents, to take down.

All things considered, it was easy to find one thirteen-year-old kid.

The car I'd seen belonged to Jaden Traeger, just like I'd thought. Jaden was twenty-one, old enough to buy liquor for his little brother and his friend. He regularly went on joyrides with Jonathan and Miles, apparently when Miles had told Andie he was innocently hanging out with his friends. The Traeger parents, realizing that both a former DEA agent and a former sheriff were breathing down their necks, coughed up the names and numbers of a few of Jaden's friends. Said friends then coughed up some of the spots the kids liked to hang out.

I went to the hangout spots one by one, looking for Jaden's car while Andie stayed home, trying Miles's number over and over. It was pretty certain I'd find them at one of the places they usually went. The question was, why was Miles's phone off, and why hadn't he come home this time?

I got my answer when I pulled up to a lookout spot off a back road where kids sometimes hung out at night. It was dark now, and the air was chill, with a damp wind blowing down from the mountains. The only car parked in the lookout spot was Jaden's.

As I pulled up, my headlights illuminating the clearing, shadows sprinted toward Jaden's car. They were going to make a getaway. I pulled my car lengthwise across the lane, blocking the other car from leaving—a classic cop move. As I got out of my car, the shadows—there were three of them—changed course and sprinted off into the trees on foot.

I was about to chase them when I noticed a fourth shadow lying on the ground.

Miles. I was suddenly sure of it.

I ran to him, turning on the light on my phone so I could see him. It was the kid I'd seen at the gas station and the liquor store. Andie's son. He was lying on his back, trying to get up and failing. Bottles were strewn in the grass around him.

He let out a moan as my light hit his eyes, and he tried harder to get up. "What the fuck, man?" he yelled at me, his teenager's voice cracking and his words slurred.

Drunk. He was drunk. They'd been drinking, and the others—maybe more experienced drinkers than Miles—had bolted when they saw me coming. Miles was too far gone to run.

I approached Miles slowly—he wasn't going anywhere—

and squatted next to him, running my phone light up and down his body. No blood. No injuries that I could see.

"Are you a cop?" Miles said, slurring again.

I didn't answer. "Are you hurt?" I asked him instead.

"Fuck you." The words were defiant, but his voice was quavering and very, very afraid.

"Answer the question. Are you hurt?" I asked again.

"I'm fine." It was half a question. His voice cracked again.

"Well, that's something." I patted his pockets—he tried to swat me away—and found his cell phone. It was dead. I flipped my phone light off and pulled up the keypad so I could call Andie. "Your bros ran off on you, man. No loyalty at all."

"I'm not telling you anything."

I tapped Andie's number, then put the phone on speaker.

"What is it?" Her wild voice came on the other end of the line.

"I found him," I said. "He's fine. Say hi, Miles."

Now the boy sounded panicked. "Is that my mom?"

"Miles!" Andie's voice was shaking with relief and fear and anger and love. "Miles, what happened? Are you okay?"

Miles made a drunken, anguished moan, so I supplied the answer. "We're out at the lookout point off Five Line Road," I explained. "They've been drinking. Miles isn't feeling too good."

"Drunk?" Andie nearly shrieked. "He's drunk?"

"I blocked Jaden's car from leaving, but they ran off into the woods instead," I said. "They'll have to walk home. We'll call the Traegers and let them know where their sons are. Or were. I don't know who the other kid was. You can tell your dad to call off the hounds."

"Granddad?" Miles cried. "You called Granddad?"

"Oh, my God," Andie said.

"Granddad will kill me," Miles cried again.

"I'm going to kill those Traeger kids!" Andie shouted. "And their parents!"

I sat, holding the phone, suddenly wondering how I'd gotten here, in the middle of this domestic drama. This really wasn't my kind of scene. I stayed quiet as Andie yelled and Miles drunkenly despaired. Then, in the light from the phone screen, I saw Miles's skin turn an alarming shade I knew all too well.

"Hold up," I said to Andie. I pushed Miles's shoulder so he was lying on his side. He started throwing up into the grass.

"I'm coming to get him," Andie said.

"Good idea," I replied, and she hung up.

I helped Miles to his hands and knees as he threw up again. Then I turned my phone light back on and tilted his head back, pushing his eyelid up and shining the light into his eyes. His pupils looked normal.

"Did you take anything other than alcohol?" I asked—the question I couldn't ask him in front of his mother. She'd been through enough.

The fight had gone out of the kid, and he shook his head. The motion made him throw up again.

"Jesus," I muttered. I let him finish, then helped him to his feet and walked him far enough away that neither of us was in his puke puddle. He'd obviously had a lot of alcohol, especially for a kid who wasn't experienced and weighed maybe eighty pounds. But he'd thrown up so much now that he'd be less sick in the morning. For as long as he lived, he'd probably never drink rum again.

There was a low wooden fence at the entrance to the lookout point, but Miles couldn't balance enough to sit on it. No way was I putting him in my car so he could puke on my upholstery. "Sit," I told him, and arranged him on the ground like a marionette, his back against the fence and his spindly legs in front of him. The breeze blew against his pasty, sweaty skin, wafting the smell of vomit away from me.

"Who are you?" Miles asked, his words slightly less slurred.

"My name is Damon," I told him. "I work for your mother at the bar."

"Like a bartender?"

"No, like a security guy."

"Did you work for my dad?"

"No, I showed up after he left." I may as well be honest. "I knew your dad when he was DEA. I worked with him."

"You're DEA?" He looked so panicked he might cry.

"Relax," I said. "If you aren't cooking meth or dealing fentanyl, you don't have anything to worry about. Now it's your turn to answer questions. Have you ever been drunk before?"

"Not really?" He said this as a question, as if I would know better than him. "The guys give me a few beers once in a while, but tonight Jaden had rum. Please don't tell my mom I told you that. *Please.*"

He was still trying to cover his ass. I should probably be mad at him—he'd worried the hell out of Andie, and probably her father, too. He'd been idiotic and irresponsible, and he was still trying to hide things from his mother.

But I looked at Miles, and I knew that kid. He was me. Andie had said his grades were slipping and she was worried. This kid had grown up with Terry as his dad, until Terry bailed on him and turned his world upside down. He was in a bad place, and the kids he was hanging out with were no help.

So yeah, I felt for Miles. But just because he was going through something hard didn't mean there were no rules. There had been no consequences for me when I was his age, and I'd gone straight off the deep end into alcohol, drugs, and fights with my brother that landed him in prison.

"I saw you shoplift at the gas station," I told Miles. "I also saw you outside the liquor store with Jonathan while Jaden went in to buy. You've been lying to your mother for at least a month, probably longer. Tell me how long."

I watched his skinny chest rise and fall as his alcohol-muddled brain tried to come up with an answer. "You saw that?" he said weakly.

"Yeah, I did. I know that things are screwed up, but you need to get your shit together. Otherwise things are going to get real hard, real soon. And I don't mean that your mother is going to ground you. I mean that you're going to get fucked over, and it will be your own fault."

He rubbed his eyes tiredly. "I like Jaden and Jonathan. They're my friends."

"Sure they are. They're on their way home now without you, and if this ever comes up, they'll say they never met you."

Miles rubbed his eyes harder. "Everything sucks," he said with all the drama of a drunk person and a thirteen-year-old combined. Then he started talking.

Most of what he said, I couldn't follow. There was something about a test that freaked him out and he thought he'd failed it. Something about a friend of his who had just gotten his first girlfriend and didn't want to hang out with Miles anymore. A convoluted story I couldn't follow about the football team, which Miles wasn't even on—he'd failed the tryouts. His father leaving with a girlfriend and not wanting to talk on the phone. His mother snooping through his stuff and accusing him of stealing cigarettes from her purse. Like when he'd thrown up in the grass, Miles tossed up everything that was on his mind in a single run-on sentence of word vomit that went on and on.

I sat in silence, letting him get it out. He didn't seem like a bad kid; he was just crushed with anxiety and apparently didn't think he could talk to anyone about it. So I let him talk.

He was winding down, his speech slowing with exhaustion, when headlights appeared and Andie's car pulled up.

"Miles!" Andie's voice cracked as she got out of the car and ran toward us. Miles looked scared, but Andie dropped to her knees and put her arms around him, squeezing him close without another word. His body stayed stiff for a second, and then he relaxed, leaning his head on her shoulder.

"Mom, I'm sorry," he said.

She hugged him tighter.

I watched them for a moment. Then, without a word, I got up, got into my car, and went home.

TWENTY

Andie

DAMON LIVED in the top apartment of a duplex on a street packed with old houses and big trees. At least, that was what I found when I went to the address he'd given me on his paperwork. Even though I wasn't paying him, I'd still made him fill out paperwork. It was the bookkeeper in me.

It was two days since the incident with Miles. I hadn't gone into work at the Wild—I'd been busy. I'd had so much to do that I'd let Damon deal with everything at the bar, alone. I'd barely even checked in with him.

Now it was early evening. I'd gone to the Wild, expecting to find Damon there, but Jimmy said he'd gone home. I'd pulled Damon's address and come here. But when I rang the buzzer for the top apartment, no one had answered. I rang it again, and when there was still no answer—and the old man in the lower apartment glared at me from his window—I walked back down the steps, not sure what to do.

He wasn't expecting me. I could call him. Maybe he was grocery shopping or running an errand; I had no idea what Damon did in his off hours, really.

Maybe he was on a date. Did he date?

I should leave, but then I realized Damon's car was in the driveway. Wherever he went, he was walking. Or someone had picked him up. His date?

Why was I so worried about Damon going on a date?

Why was I so twisted up? I really wanted to talk to him, but I didn't want to call him. What would I say? *I showed up at your door because I'm pathetic?* Undecided, I sat on the front steps of his building. I'd give it five minutes—no, ten—and then I'd take my humiliation and go home.

I blew out a breath. This was stupid. I had worked with Damon for weeks. There was no reason he should make me nervous. I wasn't nervous.

In the dimming light, I saw a figure come around the corner, and, to my embarrassment, my whole body woke up. It was Damon. He was jogging, his body moving with powerful grace and ease as his strides ate up the sidewalk. He was wearing gray sweatpants, a zip-up hoodie, and earphones. A dark vee of sweat soaked the front of the hoodie. When he saw me, his gray eyes locked on me, but his stride didn't break.

He slowed as he got to the front walk, then stopped a few feet from me. He lowered the headphones so they were hooked around his neck.

I kept my hands in my lap. He looked good, I realized. Not just hot—Damon was hot—but good. He looked healthier every day, it seemed. His body had filled out. His muscles were taut and strong. The skin on his neck was flushed with exertion and a drop of sweat trickled down the hollow of his throat. He was a perfect male specimen, standing right in front of me, and suddenly I forgot why I was here.

Still watching me from those dark-lashed eyes, Damon put his hands on his knees as if he was winded, though he didn't seem particularly out of breath. "Hi," he said.

"Hi," I replied.

He waited, but when I didn't offer anything else, he said, "Should I ask why you're sitting on my front step?"

"I came to talk to you, but you weren't home," I said.

He waited again. The breeze blew in the trees, rustling the new leaves, the air crisp and slightly damp. Something arced between Damon and me—something that had always been there, maybe. Something I didn't want to face—but wanted to grab with both hands at the same time.

He didn't look away. If he found my behavior weird, he gave no sign.

Finally, he spoke. "Andie."

"Thank you for the other night," I said. "For your help. I would have lost my mind without you."

He narrowed his eyes a little. "That isn't why you came here."

"It's partly why," I argued. "I also wanted to say that Miles and I talked. When he sobered up I didn't yell at him, and we really talked. We're going to make some changes. His teachers are letting him redo a couple of assignments to pull his grades up. We're going to look for a therapist, see if there's one he feels comfortable with. So maybe he can talk to someone while he goes through this shit with Terry."

"Uh huh." Damon's voice was flat.

"He liked you," I said. "He didn't tell me what happened really, what you two talked about. But whatever you did or said, it helped."

"That's nice."

"He's really a good kid. I mean it."

"I know."

I twisted a lock of hair around my finger, let my gaze wander past his shoulder. "I also think we should talk about the fact that our four-week trial period is up."

He was so still, his hands on his knees, the line of his back and shoulders stark in the fading light. "We should," he agreed, "but that's also not the reason you came here."

I blew out a frustrated breath. "Are we going to talk outside? Or are you going to invite me in?"

A smile touched the corner of Damon's mouth. "Andie, I'll invite you in when you tell me the real reason you came."

My pulse raced hard in my throat. "I came because we needed to talk."

"No."

I was starting to quietly panic. "I thought I should update you."

"No again."

"I was going to—"

"No again."

I stared at him helplessly. He waited. We had a silent standoff.

After a moment he said softly, "I know why you came here, Andie. I want to hear you say it."

Something unwound deep in my belly. Like someone had cut a string that was pulled too tightly, and I could practically hear the *zing!* as it snapped. I stopped panicking and I felt heat moving through me.

How did he know me so well? How did he know what I wanted when I was still trying to figure it out myself?

I said on an exhale, "I came because I wanted to see you."

Damon's eyes went dark, but he didn't move. His voice was a rasp. "You wanted to see me what?"

I'd never done this before—never talked to a man like this.

Never said these kinds of things to anyone, even my ex-husband. "Naked," I said. "I wanted to see you naked."

A muscle twitched in his jaw. "Good," he said. "That's very good. I want to see you naked, too. I always have. How much time do we have?"

I swallowed. "Miles is spending a few days with my father."

"So we have all night."

"Yes."

The smile touched Damon's mouth again. "See? That wasn't so hard. Come in."

TWENTY-ONE

Andie

I FOLLOWED Damon up the stairs to his apartment. With every step, my nerves and awkwardness fell away, and I felt more confident. More sexy. I'd never been this woman, who showed up on a man's doorstep with pleasure in mind. But with Damon, I could be that woman, and I liked it.

He let us in to his place. It was a small apartment, cozy, with a sturdy old sofa, a TV, and a functional kitchen. The back door in the kitchen opened to a small back deck and a fire escape, and through the window I could see a beautiful view of the mountains. A laptop was set up on the kitchen table, and I pictured Damon eating alone while working. There were no personal photos anywhere, no vacation shots or photos of family, but the space was still very much Damon's. His things were everywhere, his scent everywhere, and the combination of loneliness and comfort reflected his personality.

COLD DARK HEART   125

He was moving through life alone, perhaps, but he wasn't as cold as he let on.

"I need a shower," he said, pulling off his sweaty hoodie. Beneath it was a T-shirt, stuck to his torso with sweat.

I was going to say the polite thing: *Okay, I'll wait.* He didn't give me the chance. He took my hand and led me toward the bathroom.

I followed, too startled by the warm strength of his hand grasping mine. Just that touch sent warmth up my arm and through my body, and I stared at his taut arm, with the edge of the tattoo on his biceps, as he led me where he wanted me to go.

Because I was stupid with lust, it took me a minute to realize he was bringing me into the bathroom with him, where he was going to take a shower. He led me through the door, then dropped my hand and pulled his T-shirt off with one motion. He unlaced his running shoes and took them off, followed by his socks. He straightened and hooked his fingers into the waistband of his gray sweatpants, and then he paused, looking at me.

"Strip," he said.

I barely heard him. I was transfixed by the sight of his naked torso. Not just the beauty of it, the taut muscles and the dusting of dark blond hair over his chest and flat stomach. I was also transfixed by the two scars on his chest, one in the soft area below the bone of his right shoulder, the other a few inches down where the second bullet must have penetrated his ribcage. The scars were months old now, white and smooth, yet still they looked angry and painful, remnants of the horrible thing that had happened to him. It was one thing to hear someone tell you they had been shot twice. It was another to see the evidence of two bullets piercing someone's skin.

Watching my gaze, Damon stepped closer to me. Without a

word he lifted one of my hands and placed it over one of the scars. "I don't bite," he said.

His skin was warm, so warm. I was touching a man, this beautiful man, and we were going to do amazing things together for as many hours as we wanted. This wasn't Terry. I never had to touch Terry again. I never had to let him put his hands on me.

Instead, I would have Damon's hands on me. I suddenly wanted that more than anything, to feel this man's hands everywhere on me. I inhaled a breath as my body throbbed with desire. I moved my hand over his skin, feeling the soft touch of the hair there, the smooth place where the hair ended and the scar began.

Getting bolder, I ran my fingertips over the scar itself, feeling the texture and the warmth of it. Then I moved my hand to the other scar, touching that one, too. Damon stood still, letting me explore at my leisure, but the muscle in his jaw was ticking again. He was barely keeping control.

I raised my other hand and put my palm on his chest. I let my skin move over his, taking him in, letting him take in the feel of me, skin to skin. I brushed over his nipple and felt his inhale of breath. Just touching him like this was making me breathless, making heat pulse through my body and deep into my belly. I moved both hands down to his stomach, touching the hair that led down into the waistband of his pants. I stopped just short of the waistband and moved my hands to the sides, caressing his waist and the tops of his hips.

"Andie," he said softly. I raised my gaze to see his eyes on mine, dark and intent. He cupped my jaw with both of his hands and kissed me.

We melded perfectly, the kiss deepening fast, both of us leaning in. He ravished my mouth and I kept my hands on his hips, gripping him, feeling the heat and the strength beneath my hands. I wanted this. I wanted him against me, inside me, like I had never wanted anything. I was an endless swirl of need, of craving, and what I needed most was him.

He broke the kiss. "Strip," he said again, still cradling my jaw, and my hands immediately went to my jean jacket, then to the buttons of my shirt. In seconds I had both off and had stripped down to my bra. I had a split second to remember that my bra was nothing special—just an everyday bra I'd bought on sale a year ago instead of something lacy and seductive—before Damon had unhooked it and dropped it to the floor.

I inhaled as his hands cupped my bare breasts. Only two men had ever seen my breasts, had touched them, until this moment. And all of it felt right. What had happened before, and what was happening now—that this man, right this minute, would be the third person I'd give my body to. It was perfect. I let my eyes drift close as he touched me, his palms moving over my sensitive skin, over my nipples. I forgot about the fact that I wasn't a model, that I'd had a baby, which made my body less than picture perfect. I just tilted my head back and let myself feel.

Damon ran his thumbs lightly over my nipples, making me gasp, and then he leaned in and kissed the sensitive skin of my neck. "Take off the rest of it," he growled, and then he pulled away to turn the shower on.

I pulled off my ankle boots and my pants, leaving only my panties. As the steam from the shower began to fill the bathroom, Damon dropped his track pants and his underwear in one motion. He stepped forward and slid my panties off my hips and to the floor. Then he pulled me into the shower with him.

He kissed me as we moved under the water, and then we were skin to skin, our bodies fused together, our hands everywhere. The heat of the water mixed with the heat of his touch, and every nerve ending on my skin was alive. Damon kissed me deep, and he tasted so good. I broke the kiss and put my mouth on his neck, tasting his skin and the hot water, sucking on him like a wanton woman as his hands moved down my back and over my ass.

We were soaked now. Damon pressed me back against the wall of the shower, making me yelp as the cool tiles hit my overheated skin. He pressed his body into mine, his chest and hips pinning me deliciously, and I could feel him hot and hard against me. *Yes,* I thought. *This is exactly what I want. Just this, just now. I want it and I deserve it.*

I slid my hands down to his hips again, pulling him against me, the bossiest move I'd ever made with a man. I felt Damon smile against my skin.

"I need to grab a condom," he rasped.

The woman who was coming through me now, the one who had no limits, said, "You don't have to. I had my tubes tied five years ago."

Damon's body went still against mine, though he didn't move away. "Fuck, Andie, you're killing me."

"I got tested after you told me about Terry," I went on. Where had my awkwardness gone? My sense of shame? They had both vanished. I was completely shameless right now for maybe the first time in my life. "I'm clean."

He groaned, the sound mixing with the sound of the running water. "So am I. Jesus, Andie, are you sure?"

"I'm sure." I was. I pressed my hips against his, feeling the heat and power of him. I'd never been sure like I was in this moment. "This is what I want," I said to him. "What do you want?"

Damon kissed me, slow and harsh, and then he said, "I want to make you feel good. That's all I want. Just to make you feel so fucking good."

"Then do it," I whispered.

His gray eyes were serious and beautiful as they looked into mine, assessing me. Reading me. I let him see everything, all of the rawness of myself in that moment, without holding anything back.

He made a decision. He lifted one of my knees and hooked my leg around his hip so I was open to him. Then, as the hot water ran over us, he pushed inside me.

The feel of him only made my pulse pound harder and my desire more frantic. "More," I said. "I want to feel good, Damon. Please."

He obliged. He started to move, taking me against the shower wall just the way I wanted. This wasn't sweet, romantic lovemaking; Damon took me hard, his powerful body pinning mine, his biceps flexing where his arm was braced against the wall, the water running in rivulets over his muscles. I'd never had sex in the shower before, but right now it came naturally as I softened myself and opened up to him, letting pleasure wash over me. Taking what I wanted. Giving pleasure to this man, and only him.

He was so slick inside me, so powerful, that when I came I dug my fingernails into his bare back. He made a sound deep in his throat as he felt me squeeze him, and then he pounded me mercilessly for another minute until he came. Without missing a beat he turned the shower off and kissed me again, deep and just a little rough, as his arm reached out and grabbed a towel from the rack. He wrapped it around me, then dug his fingers into my wet hair.

"Don't leave yet," he said, his voice a rasp. "Stay longer."

I hadn't even thought of leaving. In fact, in this moment, you couldn't have made me go anywhere.

But Damon didn't know that. His expression was deadly

serious, as if I'd already told him, seconds after coming, that I was planning to go.

What made him think that? Why did he assume I would fuck him, then walk out the door?

"I'm staying," I told him.

Damon looked at me a moment longer, as if wondering whether to believe me. I pressed up onto my toes and brushed my lips over his mouth, reassuring him.

"All right," he said finally, the words tentative. "You're staying. I'm taking you to bed."

TWENTY-TWO

Damon

I WAS SITTING at the bar at the Wild, looking through paperwork. It was a weekday, we opened in half an hour, and Cory was loading a new keg.

The bar had improved in the past few weeks. It was all Andie's doing. She had bought new tables and chairs, getting rid of the old ones that were permanently sticky with spilled beer. A chalkboard had been put up behind the bar, listing the evening's cocktail specials. She had even brought in a band one night to play bluegrass music. We were starting to get new customers instead of the same old crusty regulars every day.

I was engrossed in the papers I was studying, so I was surprised when I heard the slide of a glass over the bar. A glass of soda and lime appeared at my elbow.

I looked up. Andie was standing behind the bar, her arms crossed and her hip cocked. Her dark hair was tied up off her neck, and for a second I just stared at her like a lion who hasn't been fed in months.

Since that incredible night at my apartment over a week ago, we hadn't been together. It was impossible. When Andie and I weren't at the bar, she was home with Miles—and the new, reformed Miles was *always* home when he wasn't at school. It was great that he was taking his second chance seriously, that he was trying hard to recoup his grades and not run wild with the Traeger brothers. But it also meant that there was no way Andie could sneak away so I could bang her senseless like I wanted to. If Miles was aiming to be a model son, then the least Andie could do was be a model mom. Which meant no sex with the help.

At work, we had to pretend things were the same as ever so that rumors wouldn't start. Andie was the boss, she was Terry's ex, and again, she needed to be a paragon of womanhood—or she at least had to appear that way. When I worked with her, I had to pretend I hadn't seen her naked, hadn't been inside her bare, hadn't had her in my shower and on my bed. I was a guy with a lot of self control, but it was very fucking hard.

I looked around. "Where did Cory go?"

"I sent him down the street to the market to pick up lemons and limes. We're out."

I'd been so engrossed, I hadn't even heard Cory leave. Andie and I were alone in the bar, at least for the moment.

"What are you reading?" she asked.

"Invoices," I said, distracted as I let my gaze travel her again. "You're wearing a dress."

"Very perceptive." But her skin flushed a little. The dress was one of those wraparound ones, with a deep vee in the neck where the two parts overlap. It fit her like a second skin, and I could see the dip of her waist and the perfect curve of her hips beneath the fabric of navy blue with small white flowers on it.

"I've never seen you in a dress before." Andie looked hot as hell in jeans, but this was something else entirely.

She shrugged, though her arms were still crossed. "I had to take Miles to meet his new therapist this morning. That's why I'm late."

"You went to meet a therapist in that?" She was wearing knee-high boots that brushed the hem of the dress. Jesus, she looked sexy. "Was he an eighty-year-old man?"

Her dark brows lowered in that way I knew so well. "You don't think I should wear this outfit?"

"I think any man under eighty who sees you in that dress is not going to be able to concentrate on Miles's mental well-being."

"Oh." Andie uncrossed her arms and smoothed the dress down her front, a gesture that was supposed to be professional but instead made the fabric pull over her perfect breasts. "He didn't seem to notice."

"Then he needs his eyes checked," I said.

She flushed again, and our gazes met. It had only been a week, but I felt like a man who has crossed the Sahara on foot since he'd last had sex with Andie English. Like a man who had been off to war for years.

"Damon," she said.

My gaze dropped to that vee between her breasts again. I couldn't help it. "Yes?"

"I want to talk to you about your employment."

I blinked, raising my gaze to her face again. "What about it?"

"I need to start paying you a salary."

"No."

She sighed gustily. "You can't just work here for free forever."

"You can't pay me, either."

"Why not?"

"Because then I'd be fucking the boss."

She blushed hard at that, the color flooding up her cheeks. I'd only said it because we were alone, and because I wanted to see Andie blush. Because she liked it—I could see it so clearly in her eyes. "That is—do *not* say that."

I smiled. "Of course, that's if I'm still fucking you. Which I'd like to be."

"Stop." She did not want me to stop. Not even a little bit.

Still, I said, "Seriously, I'm not going to be your employee, Andie. If it bothers you not to pay me, then pay me. But pay me as an independent contractor."

She frowned. "What do you mean?"

"I mean, I'm the security expert you hire to consult with you about security for the bar. I send you a bill, you pay it. Very simple."

She thought that over. "So according to you, it's okay if you're fucking your client, but not your boss?"

This woman. Just when I thought I had her pegged, she'd just blurt out a dirty word that made my blood run hot. "Just for the record," I said slowly, "I am absolutely okay with fucking my client."

Andie grabbed one of the laminated drink menus from the bar and fanned herself with it, making the tendrils of loose hair lift off her neck. "Oh, lord."

So she was just as pent up as I was. That was good to know. The woman who had gotten in the shower with me had been passionate and practically insatiable. She was still in there somewhere. I just needed to bring her out again. And we needed some damn privacy.

I had no idea what I was doing—what we were doing. I only knew that all I wanted lately was to get Andie naked again, and she seemed to want the same thing. We were two grown adults, unattached and able to make our own decisions. We didn't need much more than that.

What the hell was I waiting for? Andie was right here.

I pushed my stool back and put my papers into a stack. "I think we should have a meeting in your office."

Andie's eyes went wide and she put down the drink menu. "We can't do that."

"Why not? We meet in your office all the time."

"Because I know what you're thinking."

"I'm thinking I finally put a proper lock on that office door," I said. "I'm also thinking you're wearing a dress. I have those two thoughts. That's it."

She let out a breath, a sound that told me she was tempted. Absolutely tempted. She looked around at the empty bar and whispered, "At work?"

"At work," I replied, with confidence I didn't totally feel. It had been long enough, she was wearing that dress, and I was taking my shot. Either Andie would go for it or she wouldn't.

She went for it.

Her gaze met mine, and then she turned and walked toward the office. "Fine," she said. "A meeting."

I picked up my papers. As I followed her, Cory came back through the front door, bags from the market in his hands. "Meeting with the boss," I told him.

Cory looked completely uninterested in this news. "Okay."

As soon as the door clicked shut behind us, I turned the lock. Then I dropped my papers. Then I took Andie's face in my hands and kissed her.

She grabbed the lapels of my jacket and kissed me back. She tasted like sweet lip gloss and hungry woman. I wasted no time running my hands over her like I'd been dying to do for over a week now, since the last time I'd had her. I cupped her ass through the fabric of the dress, squeezing just the way she liked it and making her moan into my mouth. Then I backed her against the desk and lifted the hem of her dress.

"On the desk!" she whispered. She was outraged and incredibly turned on.

"Yes," I whispered back. "You'll have to be quiet when I make you come."

That made her moan again, though she bit it back so that no one would hear past the door. I was insane for her, craving her. I slid my hand into her panties and nearly lost my mind at how wet she was.

She made a little sound and squirmed against my hand, and except for the day I'd come home from a jog and found Andie on my doorstep, this was suddenly the best day of my life. I really, really liked making this woman squirm, knowing she was making those sounds because of me. I had seen her too many times when she was tense with stress, worry, and the burdens she carried every day. I had watched her keep it together for the benefit of everyone else. I wanted to be the one to make her eyes close and her head tilt back as she took a deep inhale of pleasure. I wanted to be the one to make her feel good. I wanted to be the one to make her let go.

Andie pulsed her hips up against my hand, and as I moved my thumb over her, she gasped. I pressed the fingers of my free hand lightly over her mouth, reminding her to be silent, and that seemed to turn her on even more. I was hardly the most wildly experienced guy on the planet, but I was starting to realize that even though Andie had been married, she hadn't tried very many things. She'd never experimented, taken the time and attention to figure out exactly what she wanted and liked. I had no desire to know what her sex life with Terry had been like, but I was more than happy to be the guy who over-wrote those memories with sex that was a little bit risky and actually fucking fun.

She bit the pad of one of my fingers over her lips, and then she sucked it into her mouth, and I nearly lost it. I leaned close to her ear as I stroked her. "You are so fucking sexy right now," I whispered. "You're making me insane."

Andie made a little sound in her throat and grasped for my belt buckle, undoing it.

Well. If that was what she wanted, I was all for it. I nipped her earlobe and rasped, "On the desk?"

"Yes," she whispered.

I slid her panties off while she worked my zipper. Pushing aside stacks of papers, I leaned her back to just the right angle. I parted her knees. I slid deep inside her. And then I fucked her right there on the desk in her office, her dress around her waist and her heels digging into my lower back. The desk made an alarming rocking sound, but no one came to the door.

When her body started to pulse, I put my hand over her mouth again, just hard enough to make her orgasm hit harder. And then, when we were both finished, I kissed her long and deep, on the desk with all the papers and the computer pushed aside.

The relaxed, dreamy look on Andie's face was worth every bit of risk.

I was addicted.

TWENTY-THREE

Andie

IT WAS A BEAUTIFUL DAY, one of the first really warm days of spring, as I left the café and got into my car. The Colorado sky was a clear, blinding blue with barely a cloud in sight. The landscape was starting to turn green. In the distance, the mountains stood majestic and unchanged. I'd lived in Colorado all my life, and on days like this I knew I never planned to leave.

I fished through my purse for my sunglasses. I'd just had lunch with Ginny Newtown, the owner of Newtown Brewing. It was supposed to be a business lunch to discuss the payments I was making on our account, as well as the new products Newtown was going to roll out for summer. I hadn't needed to bring Damon, since I didn't need any protection from Ginny. I'd left him at the Wild, and it was just her and me.

She'd looked me up and down when I came to our table, and said, "Hottie Bodyguard, huh? Girl, you're having fun."

"Is it that obvious?" I'd asked, pulling out my chair.

"Oh, honey." She shook her head. "Let's order."

We'd talked business for all of five minutes, and we'd spent the rest of lunch talking about...everything. Books, movies, motherhood—Ginny had a son and a daughter, both in their late teens and headed to college. We talked about the booze business and Salt Springs and house prices and where to buy the best coffee. Before I knew it, lunch had lasted two hours and my stomach ached from laughing so much.

We didn't talk about Terry. Except for that first greeting, we didn't even talk about Damon or my sex life. From one look at me, Ginny knew everything she needed to know. *I have an actual friend,* I thought with wonder as I got in my car. And as much as I hated that he still took up space in my head, my next thought was that Terry would have hated me having a two-hour lunch with Ginny, a woman who wouldn't sleep with him. He'd make nasty, belittling jokes about it—*two hours swapping makeup tips, huh? Does it really take that long to talk about lipstick?*—until he wore me down, and the next time Ginny asked me to lunch, I'd say no.

For a second I felt like screaming and crying, because fuck Terry. Fuck all the times he'd made me feel less than enough. Fuck all the years he'd taken from me. Fuck all the horrible things he'd said.

I had the feeling these moments of rage would be with me for a while, but for now, this one passed. Terry was gone forever. We were legally divorced. The West was mine, my money was mine, my decisions were mine, and my future was mine. I could have as many two-hour lunches as I wanted with whoever I wanted.

And yes, I could have hot sex with my security consultant on my desk at work. I started the car and turned on the air conditioning, because every time I thought about that wild banging session even now, a week later, my body overheated. Holy hell, that had been amazing. And risky. And fun.

I pulled out my phone and texted Damon, who was at the Wild. *Lunch went long. Everything okay?*

All good, was his reply. *New cash drawer being installed. The guys are almost finished.*

The latest upgrade at the bar was to the cash register, which until now had been opened by a simple switch. Honestly, anyone could have gotten into that thing—I had no idea what Terry was thinking. Damon was having it replaced with a proper cash drawer that could only be opened when an authorized employee was using the register, using a security code. Just one of the many things my hot security consultant was doing for me.

Since the day on my desk, we hadn't been able to get together again. It turned out that being a single mom, while also being a single woman who was having sex with a hot lover, was complicated to schedule. As it was, because of my long lunch, Miles's school day was over soon and he'd be heading home. He'd had his bicycle privileges suspended for a month because of the drinking incident, and he was taking the school bus with all of the other kids. He'd be home by four. And because we were both making an effort right now, I needed to be home at four, too.

This wouldn't be forever. Someday, Miles would earn my trust again and we'd figure out new rules so he could have some of the freedom he craved. But for now—and especially until his grades came back up before the school year ended— we both had to put the work in to make our family feel whole again.

It was important. But it poured cold water onto my sex life. It was an unsolvable problem.

As I was about to put the car in gear, my phone rang. It was my father. I stayed parked, turned off the car, and answered him. "Hi, Dad."

"Hi, honey. Where's Miles?"

He asked me this every time we talked lately, as if since the drinking incident, I was at constant risk of misplacing my son. "Since it's the middle of a school day, he's in school," I replied.

"Did he re-take the English test?"

"Yesterday. He doesn't have his marks back yet."

"I hope they're good. I want him to get into a good college."

Was it worth pointing out that at thirteen, Miles's English test marks would have nothing to do with college? No, it wasn't. Was it worth pointing out that my dad had never once suggested I go to college? Also no.

All of this should make me crazy, but for some reason, today I just shrugged it off. My dad was my dad. He and Miles loved each other a lot. That was all that really mattered. "What's this call about?" I asked.

"I was calling to remind you about the lake weekend."

"That's next weekend."

"No, it's this weekend."

I sat up straighter in the driver's seat. I knew my calendar by heart, and I definitely had the lake weekend down as next weekend. "Are you sure?"

"Of course I'm sure. The guys and I have been planning it all week. I want to pick up Miles at six o'clock on Friday."

The lake weekend was an annual thing in which a group of cops, and former cops like my dad, went to a nearby lake, three hours away, to stay in a cluster of cabins there. They went fishing and boating and went feral, coming back smelling awful. They also brought their sons.

It was a true guys' weekend, and my father had started bringing Miles last year. Miles had loved it.

I'd thought they were going next weekend, but somehow I

had the date wrong. They were going this weekend, which meant—

I was going to be home alone. All weekend.

"Of course you can pick him up!" I practically shouted at my dad. "That sounds great!"

"Are you okay, Andie? You sound overexcited."

"I am excited! For Miles. I told him the wrong date, so this is going to be a pleasant surprise for him. He's going to be so happy!"

"Well, okay." Dad still sounded confused. "Just make sure to tell him when he gets home from school. And there are a few things you need to pick up for him. Sunscreen and bug spray and such."

"I'll get right on it!" I couldn't keep the cheer from my voice. "Such good news!"

"What will you do all weekend?"

"Oh, I'll catch up on paperwork. Tax time and all. I'll wear my jammies and watch Netflix. I'll be just fine."

Smooth, Andie. So smooth. You got this.

"Better you than me," Dad grumbled. "Talk to you later."

We had barely hung up when I called Damon. He picked up right away.

"Hey, Andie." I knew from his neutral tone that he was in the bar, probably within earshot of other people. He sounded calm and businesslike.

I had the sudden urge to say something scandalous and completely filthy in his ear, to see if I could shake him. I started with: "I just heard some good news."

"Yeah?"

"I thought Miles was going away with his grandfather next weekend. I had it wrong. He's going away with his grandfather *this* weekend instead. From Friday all the way to Sunday."

There was a pause, loaded with significance. Then Damon said, "That's very good news for Miles."

He was definitely in earshot of other people. "As soon as he leaves, I'm going to get naked," I said. "I'm going to..." I wasn't any good at dirty talk. I'd never practiced. But I decided to try. "I'm going to lie in bed, and I'm going to put my hand between my legs, and I'm going to rub myself. It's going to feel so good. But I'm going to be lonely."

There was a strangled cough on the other end of the line.

"Damon?"

"I'm listening."

"I'm going to be naked all weekend. Do you plan to join me?"

"I'm pretty sure I can clear my schedule, yes."

"Good to hear it. Eight o'clock Friday night. My place."

"Got it, boss."

I hung up smiling. I had just over an hour before Miles would be home from school. I could drop by the Wild, try and get a little work done. Or I could go home early and put a load of laundry in, clean the house.

In the end, I didn't do either of those things.

I went lingerie shopping instead.

TWENTY-FOUR

Andie

MY BACK HIT the bed and I bounced on the mattress, laughing. Damon pinned my wrists and braced himself over me, his gaze taking me in.

"Very nice," he said.

The lingerie shopping had been a success. I was in a black lace teddy that hugged my body from my breasts to the tops of my thighs. It had feminine straps and almost no back. It came with matching panties that were barely more than a tiny scrap of lace. After Miles left with his grandfather, I had spent two hours shaving, waxing, and putting on just the right amount of makeup and scented lotion.

The result? Damon had been here barely ten minutes, and he was already down to his boxer briefs and was pinning me to the bed.

For tonight, I'd solved the single mom problem.

I let my gaze roam him, too. Although the desk incident had

been hot, I hadn't seen Damon naked since that night in his apartment. I devoured every inch of his skin—the muscles flexing in his shoulders as he held my wrists, the hollow of his clavicle, the octopus tattoo on his biceps, the lean line of his torso as it tapered to the waist of his boxer briefs. "Take those off," I said, my eyes on the briefs.

In response, Damon leaned down and kissed me. Deep. No one had ever kissed me like Damon did. No one tasted like Damon did. I squirmed against him as he did it, wanting to get closer. His hands held me just tightly enough that I couldn't get free, and I liked it.

He broke the kiss and let me go, moving down my body. Without a word he pushed up the hem of my teddy and hooked his thumbs into the tiny panties, drawing them down. Then he got my legs into position so he could get down to business.

I took a shaky breath. We'd done this in his apartment, on his bed. It had been amazing, and—

Oh, dear God.

The world just stopped. Every worry, every fear, every thought and plan in my head. There was only pleasure, white hot behind my eyes, firing through every nerve in my body. I moaned—I could be as loud as I wanted tonight—and gave in to it, letting the pleasure take over.

Damon went slow, torturing me. His tongue was magic— evil magic. Because it would bring me to the brink, and then it would leave me hanging again.

When I couldn't take it anymore, I pushed him off me and rolled him onto his back. It was my turn now. I hooked my fingers into his boxer briefs and slid them down. Then, without a second's hesitation, I took him in my mouth.

Damon's hips lifted from the bed as he hissed in a breath. This had never been my favorite thing to do—actually, it was my least favorite by far. Until now. Right now, with Damon, I started to understand how it could be teasing, fun, and desperately exciting. I wanted to savor him. I wanted to make him make sounds, like he'd done to me. I wanted to torture him.

I kept doing what I was doing until I felt the muscles in his hips and thighs starting to tense. Then I let him go.

"Damn, woman," he groaned, but he didn't sound angry. He sounded like he was enjoying himself.

I kissed my way up his taut stomach. I had no idea who this bold woman was, but I planned to be her forever if I possibly could. She was having a lot more fun than the old Andie had. I traced my tongue over Damon's skin, enjoying every warm, taut inch of him. Then I pulled my teddy up over my hips and straddled him, my sensitive flesh rubbing on his.

"Any objections?" I asked him.

His gorgeous gray eyes moved over me. Then he reached up and slid the straps of my teddy down over my shoulders, tugging the material down so my breasts came free. He cupped them in his hands.

"No," he said.

Oh, that felt good. Did people do this all the time? Have hot, wild sex like this? Why had I thought that this wasn't for me? That only other people got to have pleasure?

I slid over Damon again, watching him wince as he tried to keep control. I'd wasted weeks of time, I realized. If I was smart, I would have jumped him when he first walked through the door of the Wild. But I hadn't been ready. I was ready now.

I eased myself down onto him, feeling the pleasure pulse through my body. I dropped my head forward and closed my eyes, my hair falling over us. I heard the rasp of Damon's breath, felt one of his hands leave my breast and drop down between us.

It didn't take long. I leaned down and buried my face in his neck as I came, my body shaking. His hands dug into my hips as he came, too.

There was something different this time. We were in my house, my bed. We were having fun, but this was Damon. I didn't want just any man—I wanted him. Only him.

I wanted Damon Blake, and I didn't want him to leave.

As he cupped my face and kissed me, I knew with complete certainty:

I'm ready.

TWENTY-FIVE

Damon

SHE'D KILLED ME. I lay with my eyes closed, flickering in and out of a decadently satisfied doze as Andie went to the bathroom to clean up. I should probably be gentlemanly and help her, but I wasn't entirely sure my legs worked anymore.

When she got back into bed with me, the lace teddy was gone and she was naked. Her dark curls were deliciously tangled, her lips reddened. She was a living fantasy, and she had no idea.

She pulled the sheet over both of us and propped herself on one elbow, looking down at me. "Are you okay?" she asked, a smile curving her lips.

"I'm great," I said, meaning it. "I am very fucking great." I'd just been mauled by a wild woman, and I'd loved every second of it. In this moment, I was a happy man. We're a lot simpler than women think.

"Good," Andie said. "I think I should warn you about something."

"What?"

She bit her lip briefly, then plunged forward. "I was married for a long time. We're not going to talk about that. But let me just say that there are some things I never got to try. And I'd like to."

That woke me up all the way. "You want to try things? Like what?"

"I've put some thought into it. I can make a list if you want."

She had a list of sexual experiments? Only Andie. "Jesus. I think I'll have to join a gym. The running isn't going to cut it."

She nudged me with her elbow. "Well, you'd have to agree to everything first. That's why I suggested the list."

I shook my head. "I'm trying to think of something you could suggest that I'd say no to. Nothing comes to mind."

"That's very sweet. I just think, what if there's something I haven't tried yet that I'd really like? I would like to find out. But only with you."

I propped a hand behind my head and looked up at her. *It better be only with me,* I thought. What I said was, "Whatever you want, we'll do."

After all the talk of sex, *that* made her blush. "Well, I'm not done yet," she said. "I'd also like you to meet Miles."

"I've already met Miles."

"I mean meet him properly. Come for dinner, but actually get dinner this time." She paused. "That is, if you're planning to stay in Salt Springs."

I watched her closely, seeing the nervousness stealing into her expression. "You're asking me to be your boyfriend."

"I guess so. I mean—it isn't—if you're not—"

"Hold on, Andie." I scrubbed a hand through my hair, thinking. I had to be careful here. It was one thing for a woman to ask you to be in a relationship. It was another thing for that woman to want you to get to know her son. No mother took that decision lightly.

The fact that she'd suggested it meant Andie was serious.

Was I serious?

When it came to Andie, I was very fucking serious. I just wasn't sure she should be serious about me.

"What is it?" Her voice quavered. Great—I'd freaked her out. The sex had made me stupid. I needed to think, or I'd lose her forever.

"I'm not sure you know all the bad things about me," I explained. "You should have all the information before you make a decision like this."

Andie frowned. "You told me you used to do drugs. Years ago."

"I said I was an addict," I corrected her. "I was. I was addicted to drugs and alcohol, both. I sold drugs so I could make money to buy more drugs. If I hadn't quit, I would have died. I quit, but addicts are never cured. They're addicts forever. I still go to meetings here in Salt Springs."

"You do?"

I nodded. "Every Thursday night. I hadn't been for a while, but quitting smoking shook a few things loose. I needed to start going again."

"I'm not going to apologize for that," Andie said. "You needed to quit."

"You're right, I did. I just want to be clear what you're dealing with here. You also don't know everything that happened with my brother, Alex."

Now she looked surprised. "You have a brother?"

"Yes. And he hates me. Or he did for a long time. Maybe he still does. Neither of us really knows."

She tried to process this. "Okay. I'm going to need some backstory."

I didn't want to tell her. Not now, not ever. But this was Andie, and I needed to man up and tell the story. If we got serious, she'd find out about Alex sooner or later. One of the things you learn when you're a recovering addict is that shit like this doesn't go away just because you ignore it. It only gets worse.

I let out a breath, running my hands through my hair again. "When we were around twenty, Alex met a woman named Kat. They were crazy about each other. Perfect for each other. They were really happy. Everyone could see they were going to get married."

Andie sounded wary. "Okay. And?"

"And I wanted to ruin it, so I tried to sleep with Kat."

"Tried?"

"Yes, tried. She said no. Still, Alex was pissed that I was trying, which he should be. We got in a fight one night, and it got physical. He beat me up good. I could have just let it drop, but I pressed charges. He went to prison for a while."

"Oh, my God."

"Let me finish, because it gets worse. When Alex got out of jail, I told him I'd slept with Kat while he was inside. He believed me. They got divorced."

Andie's eyes were narrowed as she listened to this. "I take it your claim was a lie."

"Yes, it was. Kat never wanted me, only my brother. I've never even touched her. But I wrecked what my brother had, and I did it on purpose. And after that, he hated me. I assume Kat did, too. I hadn't spoken to Alex for thirteen years until I went to Texas to see him right before I came to Salt Springs."

"I see," Andie said. "And how did that reunion go?"

"Your guess is as good as mine. He didn't kill me. I didn't kill him. He and Kat got back together, got married for the second time. They invited me to the wedding in Italy. I didn't go."

There was a long silence. "I have questions," Andie said. "So many questions."

I tried not to wince. "Go ahead."

"Why?" her voice was surprisingly gentle. "Why did you do it? Were you in love with her?"

"With Kat?" Jesus, was that what it sounded like? That Kat was some kind of love of my life? "No. I wasn't in love with Kat. She's a great woman, don't get me wrong. She's sexy and smart and her legs go for miles."

"Okay, okay. I get it."

I couldn't help but smile a little as I looked at her face. Jealousy looked sexy on her. "You know what I mean. Kat is fantastic—for Alex. They're made for each other. I've been alone with Kat maybe twice in my life, to be honest. I don't even know her very well."

"Then why?" Andie asked. "You went to all that trouble, all that heartache. You didn't have to do any of it. Why do it at all?"

Leave it to Andie to get to the heart of it. To blow past all the theatrics and drama and ask the hardest question of all.

I swallowed. "Because Alex was happy," I said. "Because I couldn't stand it. Because I wanted what he had, and deep down, I thought I'd never have it. Because when you're as angry as I was, it's easier to tear something down than to build something. So I wanted to tear something down." I shook my head. "We didn't have much of a childhood, Alex and me. Our father hit us and our mother did nothing about it. Alex left home at fifteen and moved in with his friends. I hung out for a few more beatings, and then I left, too."

"Oh, Damon." Andie's voice was quiet, but it wasn't pitying. "That's such a burden."

"Sure it was. Drugs made it easier. Alcohol made it easier. Being an angry asshole made it easier." I looked at her face, so beautiful here in bed with me, at her soft halo of dark hair. "I've fucked up," I told her. "I screwed myself out of thirteen years with my own brother, and I still haven't fixed it. That's who you're asking to come to dinner with your son."

Andie shook her head. "You think you're the only one who has screwed up?" she asked. "I met Terry when I was twenty-one, and I fell for his line of bullshit because I had practically no experience with men. Then I got pregnant and had to marry him. And Miles wasn't a mistake—he's the best thing that's ever happened to me—but I *stayed* with Terry. I thought no other man would want me and I had nowhere else to go. Deep down, I knew that our marriage wasn't right. I knew that Terry wasn't good to me. But I chose not to face the truth because it was easier for me. I'd say that neither of us deserves Miles, but now he's had his own screwup. Maybe it's best if all three of us just start over."

I couldn't quite believe we were still having this conversation, that she hadn't kicked me out yet. "You're serious?" I asked her. "You still want me to stay?"

"Well, let's see." Her starchy tone was pure Andie. "Are you going to cheat on me?"

"Fuck, no."

"Are you going to be unkind to Miles?"

"What? No."

"Are you going to dump me and leave Salt Springs?"

"No." It was the truth. I liked this town, weird as it was. And the thought of leaving Andie—No, I was not leaving Andie.

"Well, then. I think we should have dinner." She leaned down and kissed me. She tasted like sweet, hot woman. When she broke the kiss, I saw her smile. "Congratulations," she said. "It looks like you're my boyfriend."

HOURS LATER, after a second round—we had started on Andie's list—I was in a deep sleep when I heard my phone go off.

I blinked, instantly awake. My phone wasn't ringing; it was an alarm. "Shit," I said. I rolled out of bed and found my jeans where I'd dropped them in the doorway of the bedroom. I could see the phone lighting up in the pocket. I pulled the phone out and swiped it on as the alarm continued to sound.

Oh, holy fucking hell.

I dropped the phone—it was still sounding—and dragged my underwear on. Then my jeans.

"What is it?" Andie's voice came from the bed. When she saw me throwing my clothes on, her tone was alarmed. "Damon? What is it?"

"Stay here," I said, pulling my shirt on.

"What? Where are you going?"

"To the Wild."

She sat up. "Why the hell are you going to the Wild?"

"Because the app on my phone that connects to the security system just went off," I told her. "Someone's breaking in."

TWENTY-SIX

Damon

I GOT to the Wild a few minutes after a police cruiser did, because the security system was set up to automatically notify the police of a break-in. The cruiser was parked in front of the bar in the dark, its lights flashing. I saw two flashlight beams moving as the cops from the Salt Springs PD circled the building.

I parked and approached. When one of the flashlight beams swung my way, I put my hands out from my sides. "I work for the owner," I said, loudly and clearly. "My name is Damon Blake and I'm the head of security. The system alerted my phone. I'm also former DEA."

In the pulsing lights from the cruiser, I could see that the uniform was a guy of about thirty with a trim beard. "Okay, let us check it out," he said.

"I'm trained."

"I don't think—"

"Peyton! Back here!" a voice called from the back of the building.

The cop, Peyton, turned and hurried toward his partner. I followed.

The back door of the Wild was hanging open, the door itself damaged. From the looks of the marks on the door and the frame, someone—or multiple someones—had used a crowbar. "Fuck," I said aloud. "I knew we should have replaced that door. It was on my list. I just hadn't gotten to it yet."

Both cops looked at me. "This door is alarmed?"

"Yep." I nodded toward the keypad that had recently been installed on the wall. "Our brand new system. There's a camera up there, too." I pointed above the door. "It will have recorded footage. It's got a motion detector."

The two uniforms exchanged a look. "Okay," Peyton said. "They could be in there. We're going in to check. Wait here."

They went cautiously through the door, announcing themselves as police. I itched to follow them, but I had no desire to get shot—again—when I startled one of them. So I waited.

After about fifteen minutes, both cops came back out into the alley. "What did you say your name was?" Peyton asked.

"Damon Blake."

"How long have you worked here?"

"Just over a month. Did you find anything in there?" There wasn't much cash left after the bank deposit, but I'd it locked up properly, at least. Unless this was somehow an inside job by someone with a code to the cash register.

"Can you come to our cruiser so we can see some ID?"

"What did you find?" I insisted. "Was anything stolen?"

"Mr. Blake—"

"Fuck it," I said. I pushed past them and walked into the bar. They could arrest me if they wanted.

I walked into the back hall, past the bathrooms and the

door to the basement where the furnace was. It was dark in here, so I pulled out my phone and turned the flashlight on.

Ignoring the protests of the two uniforms behind me, I walked further into the bar. Nothing broken, no blood, no dead bodies. All good so far. The door to the office had marks on it where someone had started with the crowbar, but the door had held fast. *That's my new lock, assholes. Nice try and go fuck yourselves.*

Still, everything about this was odd. Both the keypad and the bubble of the camera lens were visible at the back door, an obvious indication that there was an alarm system that would alert the cops. But the thieves had broken in anyway. They would have to know that they'd get caught on camera and that they'd have a few minutes, tops, to get in and out before the police showed up.

That made it a smash-and-grab, which was the most common form of robbery. Most thieves aren't doing an *Ocean's Eleven*-type heist; they're just looking for even a few hundred bucks to buy their next gram. People wonder why someone would break into their car just to lift a few dollar bills and some old CD's. It's because to an addict, even a few bucks gets them closer to the only goal they care about.

But if this was a smash-and-grab, the obvious target would be the cash register or some of the expensive bottles of booze on the top shelves behind the bar. Sure, there was a chance that cash was kept in the office, but given only a few minutes before being caught, getting into the office would be slow, while using the crowbar on the cash register would be fast. Which was why I could see they'd run out of time before they got the office door open.

But a quick look at the cash register showed that no one had even tried to touch it. Which meant these guys were targeting something. Which meant—

I swung my light and saw that the door to the storeroom was open.

They'd used the crowbar here, too. The door was smashed open, much like the back door was. So this was what the thieves were targeting.

The two cops had followed me into the bar, their flashlights moving as they approached. "Mr. Blake, you need to come with us."

"What did they take?" I asked. Without touching anything, I stepped to the storeroom doorway and looked inside. "Oh, shit."

The storeroom had been ransacked, but that wasn't the problem. The problem was that the two extra crates of Sheffer whiskey that I'd noticed weeks ago were gone from the top shelf. One had been taken. And the other had fallen to the floor, presumably fumbled when the cops had arrived.

The crate had broken open.

And spilled all over the storeroom floor was fine, white powder.

TWENTY-SEVEN

Andie

"ARRESTED?" I shouted into the phone. "Damon has been arrested?"

"Not arrested," my father said. "Detained for questioning."

I looked at the clock over the stove. It was seven a.m.; Damon had left for the Wild just before four, vowing he would call me as soon as he knew what was going on.

I'd sat in a tortured suspense until he'd finally sent me only a brief text: *Someone broke into the storeroom. There were drugs in the Sheffer whiskey crates. I have to explain to the cops.*

I'd tried calling, but he hadn't answered. So, in a panic, I had done the only thing I could think of: I called Dad.

Now Dad was filling me in, based on what his fellow cops had told him. Miles was with the rest of the group, getting ready for a canoe outing, and Dad was calling me from the lodge, the only place at the lake with reliable cell phone reception.

"That's crazy," I said. "Damon isn't the one who broke in to the Wild. Why are they questioning him? And why has he been there for three hours?"

"Andie. How well do you know this guy?"

How to answer that one? *I know what his skin tastes like. I know how his hands grip me while I come.* "He's worked for me for weeks," I said instead to my dad. "You did a background check on him yourself before I hired him. Remember?"

"Yeah, but how well do you know him? And—wait a minute. How do you know he wasn't the one who did the break-in?"

Busted. Damon had been in bed with me. I couldn't think of a good enough lie, and my dad, with his dad instincts, was much faster than I was.

"You're *involved* with him?" He sounded almost disgusted. "Jesus, Andie. I swear I don't know what to do with you."

"You don't have to do anything with me," I shouted into the phone. "I'm thirty-five. I can see who I want. And you'll have to get used to it, because Damon and I are dating."

"Don't you think it's suspicious?" Dad shot back. "This guy shows up out of nowhere, looking for a job. You hire him. He romances you somehow, blinds you. Suddenly there's heroin being kept in the storeroom. It hasn't crossed your mind that this guy is using you?"

"To traffic drugs? He was DEA!"

"Andie." Now he had his condescending cop's voice, the one that said *You know nothing.* "Who else would know more about how to traffic drugs without getting caught than the DEA?"

I was silent for a long moment. Static crackled over the line.

"I'm glad you're finally listening to me," Dad said. "Try to use some sense. The Salt Springs PD know what they're doing. There could be a situation, with this guy trafficking drugs

COLD DARK HEART   161

through the Wild and someone else stealing them. It could be a turf war."

I closed my eyes. "What do you recommend I do?"

"Cooperate. The cops will probably knock on your door within the next half hour, wanting to question you. Answer honestly, and tell them everything. Don't try and save your boyfriend. If he's dirty, he's dirty."

"Fine," I said. "Thanks, Dad."

"Miles and I will be home tomorrow around dinnertime."

After we hung up, I put the phone down. For the first time in my life, I was completely confident. I was facing the truth head-on instead of hiding from it. I was ready to solve a problem instead of pretending it didn't exist.

The first thing I knew was that Damon wasn't trafficking heroin through my bar.

But I knew who was.

It was like Dad said: *Who else would know more about how to traffic drugs without getting caught than the DEA?*

The answer was so obvious it stared me in the face.

Terry.

TWENTY-EIGHT

Damon

SOMETIME DURING THE fourth hour of questioning, the door to the interview room I was sitting in opened and a very, very large man came in. He was well over six feet tall and probably weighed three hundred pounds. He was black and bald. He was wearing a suit and carrying a briefcase.

"My name is Aldous Peters, and this man is my client," he said calmly to the two cops who were questioning me. He pointed to me. "Mr. Blake is no longer talking. In fact, I sincerely hope he hasn't talked at all."

I was confused, mostly because I was so tired. But only briefly. I hadn't called a lawyer, but someone had. Only one person came to mind.

Andie, I thought, *I owe you big.*

There was bickering between the lawyer and the cops. I tuned it out. I would have opened a vein and dripped blood all over the table for a cigarette. I was also hungry, and I wanted to see Andie.

Aldous moved into the room and sat next to me. The cheap folding chair groaned alarmingly under his weight, but it held.

"Charge my client and read him his rights, or let him go," Aldous said. "I'll wait." He pointed one large finger at me. "You be quiet."

I shrugged and kept my mouth shut. Who was I to disobey?

Thirty minutes later, Aldous and I were walking out the front door of the Salt Springs police station, and I was free as a bird. I took out my phone and scrolled to Andie's name to call her.

"She's with the police right now," Aldous said, seeing what I was doing. "They questioned her at her house, and they're probably going to the bar to do a walk-through so she can identify if anything is missing."

"Oh. Okay." I texted her instead. *Thank you for the lawyer.* She didn't reply.

"Mr. Blake," Aldous said. "What did you tell the police during questioning?"

"After my name? Not a damn thing." I put my phone back in my pocket. "I've been in dozens of interviews just like that one, only on the other side of the table. I know how they go. So I invoked my right to remain silent."

"Well, you did something right, then." Aldous looked me up and down critically. "You're too skinny. Let's go have breakfast."

He took me to a diner, and we ordered bacon and eggs, which was the only item on the menu. The bacon was crispy and the eggs were buttery but not greasy. I was suddenly ravenous. It turns out a night of wild sex with the woman you're crazy about, followed by robbery and questioning by police makes a man hungry.

"So," Aldous said as he dug into his own plate in our vinyl booth. "Tell me what's going on."

I swigged much-needed coffee and put my thoughts in order. In my long stretch of sitting in silence, listening to the police and not answering their questions, I had finally put the pieces together. "I've been stupid," I told him. "It's been in front of my face the whole time."

"Please explain."

"The Wild is being used, at least partly, as a drug front. My former colleague in the DEA, Terry, is part of it. That slick asshole from Sheffer whiskey is a partner. Terry gets the stuff in, and it gets stored and disguised in Sheffer whiskey crates. There's nothing strange about those crates going back and forth between the bar and the distillery. My guess is that somehow Sheffer is the guy who is moving the stuff to dealers. Money is laundered by both businesses. Everyone wins."

"Hmm," Aldous said. "Where does Ms. English fit into this scheme?"

I had to put my fork down because a wave of rage threatened to overtake me for a second. "She doesn't. She's innocent. Terry left her, left the state—it probably got hot for him here. He left her the bar, even signed it over to her so she'd be holding the bag. He left her sitting on top of a fucking drug ring without her knowing it. She could have been hurt. She could have been killed."

Aldous let that sink in. He didn't look pleased about it either. "That man always was a piece of shit."

"How do you know Andie?"

"I don't know her myself, but my colleague is her divorce lawyer. She called him looking for a referral, and he sent her to me. I know a good amount about that divorce. A man who abandons his wife and son is pretty damned worthless."

"She deserves better," I said. "Much better."

He gave me a look that said I was as transparent as glass.

I shrugged. I wasn't going to deny how I felt for Andie. Not to him, and not to anyone.

"Okay," Aldous said. "Who robbed the place? A rival?"

I shook my head. "Not a rival. It's too small a score."

"Mr. Blake, there was approximately fifteen thousand dollars' worth of heroin on the floor of that storeroom."

"It was a risky robbery," I said. "I already gave the cops access to all of the files from the security system, including the camera footage. No operation worth the name sends guys to do a smash-and-grab on camera for fifteen grand. What we saw last night was someone small-time. My guess is someone either Terry or Sheffer pissed off. Likely one of the Wild's former employees. I was in the middle of profiling a few of them, and a lot of them were shady. They also either quit or were fired when Terry left."

Aldous dabbed his mouth with a napkin. "Fascinating. Do you have any proof for any of it?"

"Proof isn't my problem," I said. "I'm not a cop anymore. I don't have to have proof. I get to just *know*. If the Salt Springs PD want proof, they'll have to gather it."

"And where do you fit into this little puzzle, Mr. Blake?"

I shook my head. "I just walked into it somehow. I can't figure it out. Terry offered me a job, and then he left town before I got there. I don't know what role I was supposed to play."

I didn't care, either. Terry had put Andie and Miles in danger. He was going to go down, and if at all possible, it was going to be because of me.

Aldous's expression was skeptical. "Be that as it may, right now the Salt Springs PD has you as their top suspect. They really do not like you."

I took a bite of bacon. "I'm the new guy in town. I made

some calls that overstepped my place as a civilian. And I'm a former Fed. Cops hate Feds."

"This doesn't seem to concern you," Aldous observed. "Listen. Just don't get arrested, and my job is easy. Understand?"

TWENTY-NINE

Andie

SATURDAY WAS A MESS. I spent a long time at the Wild with the police, looking carefully through everything to identify if anything outside the storeroom had been moved or stolen. I had to call the staff and tell them we were closed for now, because we couldn't open with our back door smashed in. There was insurance paperwork to fill out.

Damon and I texted. Aldous had sprung him from the police station, and he went home to shower and change. I wanted to see him so badly, but when he was finally on his way to the bar, the police asked me to come to the station to sign an official statement. So I did that while Damon and Jimmy picked up plywood and did a quick-and-dirty patchup job on the Wild's back door, enough to keep the riffraff out until the door could be replaced.

The whole thing was exhausting, I didn't eat, and by the time I headed home at last it was near dark and I was shaking. I wanted my home and my pajamas. I wanted food. I wanted Damon. I also wished, selfishly, that Miles was home—though I knew it was best that he wasn't here. I knew exactly who was behind all of this, and besides being stressed out, I was furious. It wasn't good for Miles to know exactly how much I hated his father right now.

I had just walked in my front door and taken off my shoes when my phone pinged with a text. It was Damon. *You home?*

Yes, I replied.

His next message was brief, but it lifted my spirits: *Five minutes.*

It was even less than that when I heard his car park behind mine in the driveway. I didn't even wait for him to come to the door. I walked out to the front porch to greet him.

He came up the walk in the twilight and my chest tightened. He was wearing worn jeans and a dark gray hoodie, zipped up. His dark blond hair was clean and mussed, his beard dark on his jaw. When he was on the front step below me, we melted into each other without a word. I slid my arms around his neck and buried my face against his skin and the clean fabric of his hoodie. I felt his arms come around my waist, holding me so tightly he lifted me a little off my feet. We stood like that for a long moment while I soaked him in, the scent and the warmth of him, his solid body against mine, the beat of his heart. I felt the tension inside me begin to loosen.

His hand stroked my hair and he bent to kiss my temple. "You got this, Andie," he said.

I made a strangled sound in my throat. Not because I didn't believe him, but because I did. Because Damon knew it. Because he didn't feel the need to take over and push me aside, but instead he was here to actually support me. He was my rock, and he had been from the minute he'd first walked through the door of the Wild. Whether he wanted to be or not.

Eventually, though I was clinging to him hard, he pulled back enough to cup my jaw and gently kiss me. "You okay?" he asked.

"I have a headache and I'm hungry."

"We can fix that." His gorgeous gray eyes were fixed on mine, their expression serious. "We need to talk."

"I know."

"About how someone put a lot of drugs in your bar. Someone who wasn't me, by the way."

"I know it wasn't you," I said.

"That's good." His hands rubbed down my back, and I felt warmth start to move through me, familiar and exciting. It was crazy, but I wanted Damon naked. I wanted the reassurance of his skin against mine, his weight on me.

But he was right—we needed to talk first.

"Come inside," I said to him. "We can—"

"Andie!"

I froze. I knew that voice, and so did Damon. His body went tense under my hands.

We turned. A car was parked at the curb—a shiny silver rental car. Terry had gotten out and was walking toward us across the grass.

He was tanned. He'd had a haircut, and his dark hair was cut close to his scalp. He was wearing chinos and a long-sleeved baby blue shirt. The color was weird on him, the shirt had a breast pocket that was probably supposed to be stylish, and the fabric stretched awkwardly. I realized it was because Terry was thicker around the middle than he had been when he left. His expression was nasty.

"Well, don't you two look cozy?" he said. "Blake. I see you're fucking my wife."

Damon moved fast. He didn't say a word and he didn't give a warning. Like quicksilver, he was out of my arms. He grabbed

Terry by the lapels of his ugly shirt and maneuvered him back-
ward with perfect control while Terry windmilled his arms. He
shoved my ex-husband back against his car with a smack that
could be heard two doors away.

"Say that again," Damon said.

"Get your hands off me, man!" Terry yelled.

"Say it again."

There was that ice-cold reserve I'd seen before. Damon
wasn't yelling; his face wasn't even red. His gaze had gone
blank and he held Terry easily while Terry, who had been
pretty fit for as long as I'd known him, tried to wrench away.

"This is fucking assault!" Terry yelled.

"Damon," I said. I wasn't worried about Terry's well-being,
but if the neighbors saw this and called the police, Damon
would be in trouble again. I didn't want him to spend another
day at the Salt Springs police station.

Damon paused for a brief second at the sound of my voice,
and then he let go of Terry. Terry smoothed down his ugly baby
blue shirt. "You always were fucking nuts," he said.

"What are you doing here, Terry?" I asked.

Damon pulled his phone from his back pocket. "He's trespassing," he said, tapping his phone to life with his thumb. "I
think we should call the cops."

"I'm not trespassing," Terry barked at him. "This is my
house."

"It's *my* house," I corrected him.

"Yeah, because I gave it to you."

"Correction. You gave it to me and your son."

Terry's face went red. He wasn't here to see Miles, of
course. He hadn't even asked about him.

Damon still held his phone in his hand. "Do you want me
to call the police, Andie?"

I shook my head. He put his phone away.

Terry held up his hands. "Look we got off on the wrong foot here. I'm not here to start a fight. I heard there was a break-in at the Wild, and I came to see if I could find out what's going on. Maybe help catch the guys."

I didn't need to look at Damon to know what he was thinking. Since the break-in was just over twelve hours ago, Terry had gotten on a plane from Florida pretty fast. "How did you know there was a break-in?" I asked.

"I heard it from a cop I know."

I stared at him, my stomach sinking. He was lying. He was lying, and I knew it because I recognized that tone of voice, that facial expression, the way he tilted his chin up. It was the same way Terry had talked all those times he'd told me he'd worked late or spent Saturday night with drinking buddies. All those times that he'd been with someone else, and he'd been lying to me.

Why did that still hurt? It wasn't fair. It wasn't because I was still in love with Terry, if I had ever been. Maybe it hurt because of the humiliation of knowing just how often I'd been fooled.

Or maybe it was because I knew now that the Andie I had been then deserved better, and she'd never known it herself.

Damon, as always, read my reaction, though he showed no emotion in his gray eyes. "Get the fuck out of here, man," he said to Terry, his voice harsh.

"No," Terry said. "I need to talk to you."

Damon's eyebrows went up. "To me?"

"Yeah, to you." He turned to me. "Andie, go in the house. This is between Damon and me."

Oh, now I was pissed. "Absolutely fucking not."

"Go in the house," Terry said again. "We're going to talk."

"On the driveway?" Damon asked.

"Yeah, on the driveway. That way you can't beat the shit

out of me without the whole neighborhood witnessing it. Don't lay a hand on me, Blake. I'm warning you."

"So talk," I said.

There was a moment of standoff between Damon and Terry. Then Damon shot a glance at me. "Andie, please go into the house while we discuss this."

I swallowed. So that was how it was going to be. There was another long moment of silence.

Then I turned, walked into the house, and closed the door behind me.

THIRTY

Damon

AS I WATCHED Andie close the door, my heart sank. She went into the house without a word, and then she was gone.

I turned back to Terry. Maybe I had sunk the best thing that had ever happened to me; maybe I hadn't. But right now I had to focus.

"What the fuck, man?" I said to him. "This is all your fault. Your operation is sloppy."

Terry blinked. He didn't look so good. Sure, he had a tan and an ugly shirt that probably cost a lot of money. But there were creases around his eyes that weren't there the last time I saw him, and his jawline was getting soft. When we were DEA, he'd been a guy who could easily pick up women—and he had. Now he just looked like any other middle-aged white guy on the planet.

He didn't answer me, so I spoke again. "Which former employee did the break-in? Was it Howell?"

"That fucking guy." The words seemed to come out of Terry's mouth before he could think it through. "He was always trouble. He was so mad when I turfed him. Now he thinks he's getting revenge."

I nodded. I'd actually taken a wild guess—Chris Howell was one of the Wild's former employees that I'd been looking into. He had a few arrests under his belt for possession and driving a stolen car. His social media showed a guy who liked to take selfies in front of a gym mirror and brag about getting pussy. In other words, exactly the kind of idiot who would take a stupid risk for some heroin and think he was getting a big score.

"You need to surround yourself with people you can trust," I said. "How many times did we see that in our line of work? Hiring him was a rookie mistake."

"Fuck off," Terry said. "He was useful for a while." He rubbed his face, as if he was suddenly tired. "I have everything under control."

"Do you?" I asked. "I figured out most of it, no thanks to you. You get it in, Shaffer moves it. Do you think Shaffer will talk?"

"No way." Terry dropped his hands. "He's solid."

I doubted that. From what I'd seen of Shaffer the whiskey asshole, he'd roll over to the Feds and give up Terry if it would save his own skin. We Feds had dealt with guys like him all the time.

"Okay then," I said. "Maybe you'll skate through this. What I can't figure out is where I fit into it. Why did you hire me, then skip town?"

"I was gonna bring you in," Terry said magnanimously. "I knew the DEA had cut you loose, and I knew you'd been in the business before you became a Fed. I figured you'd be interested in a new career. So I sent you that email. Then you didn't show up, and it got a little hot for me here, so I couldn't wait. I left."

"You signed the bar over to Andie."

He shrugged. "Just establishing some distance. I still had access to the Wild and I could use it whenever I wanted. I had lots of copies of the keys. Until you screwed that up."

Right. When I'd installed the security system with the keypads, I'd locked Terry out of his own business. The bad security and crappy locks at the Wild had been intentional. "So how did the product get into the storeroom?"

He looked at me like I was stupid. "Sheffer's delivery guys."

I nodded. When a delivery from Sheffer Whiskey was dropped off, it would be accepted by whoever was working at the Wild. "It was still a risk, though, if you don't have inside guys. Someone could have opened one of those crates."

"Yeah, well, sometimes you take a risk in business. I was hoping you'd clue in and cover my ass, Blake. But instead you got one whiff of Andie and fucked me over."

THIRTY-ONE

Andie

THERE WAS silence for a moment after Terry said that. I held my breath.

I was standing at the side of the house, in the shadows. When I had gone inside, I had gone straight to the back door and out to the back yard, then around the house. I had stayed quiet. I wanted to hear this, and no one was going to tell me no.

That Damon had even tried was painful. But I would think about that later.

Now I waited, wondering whether Damon would take Terry's bait. Wondering what he would say.

"What are you talking about?" Damon's voice was calm. "You didn't want her. You made that clear."

"Still, there's a code," Terry complained. "You, banging my ex? It's weird."

"It would have been different if you would have just told

me what was going on," Damon said. "I would have bought in. As it was, I had to spend the whole morning getting interrogated by the local Deputy Dawgs."

Terry's voice was amused. "You were a Fed for too long, Blake. I know you didn't say anything."

"Still, it wasn't fun."

"Just ride it out and we can make something work, okay? I have to change a few things around with the business. Be patient. The money is good, and the product is good, too. You can try it and you'll see. It's premium stuff, straight from Colombia. We don't cut it with cheap shit. We keep it pure."

"That, I'm interested in."

My stomach twisted. What was he talking about? Heroin? He'd been so careful, so dedicated to being sober. Was he telling Terry the truth, or was he lying?

"I thought you might be," Terry said. "Just keep your mouth shut and let me deal with this."

"What about Andie?" Damon asked.

I felt my breath freeze in my throat.

"Cut her loose," Terry said, as if I was someone he'd barely met instead of the mother of his son. "She's not worth the trouble. What were you gonna do, settle down and have babies?"

My eyes got hot. *Fuck you, Terry. Fuck you.*

Then Damon's voice came, calm and cold. "Of course I wasn't going to settle down. I was just having some fun."

It was like a stab to the gut. On some level, I knew that Damon was probably lying to get Terry to talk. I knew that Damon had been a different man with me than the one I was hearing now.

And on another level, that didn't matter. After thirteen years with Terry, listening to him tell me that the idea of any man liking me was a joke—it hurt. It fucking hurt.

I couldn't help it.

"Dump her," Terry said. "There are a lot of women who are more fun than she is. Trust me."

I heard Damon sigh. "Sure there are. Just get the fuck out of here. And for God's sake, lie low."

Terry snorted. "No one knows I'm here, man. Even my girl-friend thinks I'm on a golf trip for a couple of days. I'm at the Radisson at the Denver airport. As anonymous as it gets. Keep your mouth shut, asshole. I'll be in touch."

There were footsteps, the slam of a car door. A car—presumably Terry's—drove away. Then I heard Damon blow out a breath.

"I take it you heard all that," he said.

For a second, I didn't want to move. I wanted to go back in the house, get my things, and get away. I wanted to run.

But screw that. I was here now, and apparently Damon had known I was listening all along. So was all of that bullshit for Terry's benefit, or mine?

I made myself come out of the shadows and step onto the driveway. I looked at the man I'd come to trust, maybe even to love. The man I'd asked to come into my life and be in a rela-tionship with me, for better or for worse. The man I'd grown to rely on.

The man I'd thought would never talk about me like he just had.

He was still, his gaze on me. Our eyes met, and I couldn't read his expression. I couldn't read it at all.

Damon reached into the pocket of his hoodie and took out his phone. He held it up, and when the screen lit up I saw an app that was recording audio. He must have activated it when he'd pulled out his phone, threatening to call 911. He turned it off now. "I got everything," he said. "One thing that hasn't changed about Terry is that he's stupid as fuck."

I still didn't speak. I couldn't. So he'd said all of those things to keep Terry talking, because he was recording him. That explained it.

But I kept hearing Damon say, *Of course I wasn't going to settle down. I was just having some fun.*

Lies, maybe. Probably. But the words still cut. They weren't just spoken today; they had been spoken to me year after year. By Terry. By my dad, even. *You're nothing special. You aren't sexy. You aren't important. You aren't capable of running a business. Who would look twice at you?*

"Did you buy any of that?" Damon asked. His voice was cold. "Did you believe it? Even for a second?"

I felt my shoulders slump. I didn't know how to answer the question. I didn't believe it, and yet I did. "Damon," I said, my voice coming out soft.

"He wouldn't have talked while you were standing there. That's why I sent you inside. You know that, right?" Damon said. I didn't reply. "Right?"

"I didn't think you were telling the truth." I forced the words out. "But it was hard to listen to."

His expression changed, and for a second he looked hurt. Then he shut it down, and his eyes were colder than ever.

He took a step back, toward his car. "Right," he said. "I'll just go."

Was I supposed to make him feel better? I had no energy for that. I had no energy for anything. I was confused, overwhelmed, and I felt like someone had put a fist in my gut. "Maybe that's best right now," I said.

Damon nodded. He pulled out his keys and opened the driver's door of his car. "I'm gonna go bust your ex-husband for drug trafficking," he told me, his voice businesslike. "I'll talk you sometime, I guess."

I watched him go, and I didn't stop him.

And I wondered if he would keep driving, leaving all of this behind. Leaving this mess, my bar, and me. I wondered if Damon would just keep going, getting as far away as he could possibly go.

THIRTY-TWO

Andie

Two weeks later

I lowered myself onto a barstool and scrubbed my hands over my face. I was bone tired. "Jimmy," I said. "I think I'd like a beer."

From his position behind the bar, where he was breaking up a bag of ice, Jimmy paused. "Huh. Are you sure about that?"

I thought it over. "Yeah, I think I am."

Why not? I owned a bar, after all. Granted, it was a bar that had been closed for two weeks because it was the center of a drug trafficking investigation. I'd been questioned repeatedly by various levels of local and federal police, as had my employees. I'd almost lost my liquor license, though with the help of Aldous Peters, I had pulled that particular iron out of the fire. I'd also dealt with the fallout of my ex-husband being arrested on drug trafficking charges. The CEO of one of my suppliers, Shaffer Whiskey, had also been arrested, and tax evasion charges were starting to land on top of the criminal ones. My bar had been all over the news in Salt Springs for the worst possible reasons. I'd hardly had a few hours' sleep in the past two weeks.

So, yeah, maybe just this once I could have a drink.

"A beer, huh?" Jimmy still sounded skeptical. We were preparing for the bar to finally reopen tomorrow. Calling the staff back in for paid work was one of the few high points of the last little while.

The other ray of goodness, strangely enough, was Miles. Considering his father was now a federal criminal, my son was taking it well. He was going to see his new therapist. He was spending time with his friends—the good ones—playing video games and soccer. His teachers were understanding about the shit he was going through. And best of all, he was leaning on me—just a little, and reluctantly, but enough. Enough for me to know that he'd tell me if he felt like he was drowning instead of hiding things from me.

In return, I gave him space and privacy. We navigated it fresh every day, but we were navigating it.

I was proud of that. Then I remembered that I hadn't seen or heard from Damon Blake for two weeks, and I wanted that beer.

"What kind of beer do you like?" Jimmy asked, surveying our taps.

"I don't know. You pick one."

"Hmm. I think an IPA will be too strong. Too hoppy."

"Is that an IPA?" I pointed at one of the taps. "It has an owl logo. I like it."

"That's a stout. You're not ready for stout." Jimmy shook

COLD DARK HEART   183

his head. "You own a bar, and you're choosing your drink by the logo. Please don't ever drink without my assistance."

"You have a deal. Pick something for me. I want to get nice and drunk."

Jimmy's gray eyebrows went up and down in surprise, but this time he didn't comment. He poured me exactly half a pint of beer and slid it toward me.

"This isn't going to get me drunk," I complained.

"With your tolerance, it might. Drink it and I might give you more."

"This isn't fair," I said. The women in movies, TV, and books always got drunk when they were unhappy. They also ate ice cream straight from the tub, which I wasn't ready for yet. I would start with drinking, but instead of a sophisticated martini or something, I had to drink half a pint of pale, watery beer.

I lifted the glass and took a deep swig. It tasted all right, I supposed. Still, I was going to have to drink a lot of it if I wanted to get drunk into oblivion.

I was still psyching myself up when Jimmy said, "Call him."

I sagged, putting my forehead in my hands and my elbows on the bar. I had a sharp pang of missing Damon, a pang I felt a hundred times per day. "Is he even in town?" I asked.

"He's in town. He hasn't gone anywhere. I talk to him almost every day. He's as miserable as a mangy dog, by the way."

This didn't make me feel better. Damon was miserable because of me. He was also in the middle of a drug trafficking investigation, indirectly because of me. If he hadn't met me, Damon would be much better off.

"If you don't mind me asking," Jimmy said carefully, "what did you do to him?"

It was so hard to explain. "I didn't trust him," I said. "I should have, but—I don't know. It was a really low moment. And I let him go."

Jimmy was silent so long I raised my head and looked at him. He was standing with his arms crossed, a look that was both sad and thoughtful on his face.

"If you tell him to go, he'll go," he said. "If you tell him to stay, he'll stay. He's like a trained Doberman, that guy. Dangerous, but he only has one master. That's you. He'd do literally anything you say."

The words hit me like punches. I remembered standing at the side of the house, listening to Damon negotiate so easily with Terry. Listening to him say he was interested in the drugs. Listening to him agree to dump me because I wasn't any fun.

He was acting. I knew that. I *did*. And still, every word had hit the most tender parts of me, the parts that Terry had spent years tearing down. Those were the parts Damon had slipped past my defenses to touch. I had needed space and time not to feel anything. Just for a little while.

In doing that, I had no idea if I'd wrecked my chances with the best man I'd ever met.

"It was so stupid of me," I said to Jimmy. "The only thing I want is Damon back. And I don't know how to fix it."

"You can fix it by calling him and telling him to come over here," Jimmy said.

I kept my head in my hands, my gaze trained down at the bar top. "And then what? Tell him how pathetic I am?"

"You sure don't look pathetic to me," Jimmy replied. "You know you turned this place around, right? Anyone else would have closed it down and we all would have lost our jobs. Last time I checked, you didn't have anyone doing all that for you. You did it yourself."

He was right. As much as I missed Damon—and I missed

him horribly, all the time—I had to admit that in some ways, these weeks had been good for me. It had gone a long way to rebuilding my confidence when I solved problem after problem on my own. I'd had to take out loans to float the bar, which meant bank meetings and paperwork. Now the Wild was in debt, but unlike Terry, I'd made a payment plan. It wasn't easy, but I could handle this. I *had* handled it. On my own.

Still, I had liked those days when Damon drove me to meetings and I bounced my ideas off him. I liked those hours we'd spent in the car, and the hours we'd spent coming up with improvements for the Wild. And the hours we'd spent in bed.

I *really* missed the hours we'd spent in bed. I was a competent woman now, but I was back to being a sexless one. A woman who did nothing but work and take care of others, including her son, her dad, and her employees. I was back to having no one to take care of me.

And Damon, I assumed, was back to having no one to take care of him, either. Was he eating enough? Was he still off cigarettes, or had he gone back to them? Had he gone back to any of his other vices? Was he going to AA meetings? Did he need a job? He was supposed to be my consultant, but he hadn't sent me an invoice. Did he need money?

Was he going to find someone else? Some woman who would look after him and let him look after her? Someone who wasn't me?

I took another deep swig of my beer, draining the glass. Jimmy was right. I should call Damon. Just woman up and say I was sorry and I wanted him back if he would have me. I wondered if I should apologize while wearing the black lace teddy, or if that was too much. Shit, I had no idea how to do any of this. I'd call Ginny for an emergency lunch and take her advice. She'd know what to do.

I looked up from my cloud of gloom to see Jimmy putting

his phone in the worn back pocket of his jeans. "Welp," he said, "we're all set for tomorrow. Want me to lock up?"

"No, I'll do it." We'd had the back door replaced. The alarm system Damon had set up worked perfectly. So perfectly, in fact, that it had caught footage of the two men who had broken down the door and taken the heroin hidden in my storage room. They'd worn baseball caps and hoodies, but the camera still caught one man's face as he used his crowbar on my door. He was a disgruntled employee who had worked for Terry when he was the owner. He'd known just a little too much about Terry's side business, and after he was fired, he'd decided he wanted in. He'd been arrested, and it had taken him about thirty seconds to turn on his friend.

So they weren't coming back. There was no reason to anymore, since there wasn't much to steal at the Wild now except for the nice whiskey on the top shelf. Whiskey that was definitely not Shaffer brand.

There would always be some undesirables in this part of town, but it wasn't late and I was safe here. "Go home," I said to Jimmy. "Thanks for the help. And for the therapy session. You're a good listener."

"It's in my bartender DNA," Jimmy said with a wink. He put on a jean jacket that was almost older than he was. "Don't hit that lager too hard if you're going to drive home."

"Okay," I said.

"But if you're getting a ride, you can have as much as you want."

I frowned. "Why would I have a ride?"

He shrugged. "No particular reason I can think of. Keep the front door open for a few more minutes, okay?"

"What? Why?"

He smiled. "For a smart lady, you need a little help sometimes. G'night."

I watched him go, the back of my neck tingling. Something was up. The bar was quiet; I was the last one here. I wandered to the back and checked that the back door was locked—a habit. But I didn't lock the front door, just as Jimmy had asked. I couldn't have said why.

I came back to the front room and walked behind the bar, grabbing my empty glass. If my project for tonight was to get drunk like a heroine in the movies, maybe I should get going.

There was a soft click as the bar's front door opened and closed.

I looked up to see Damon standing in the doorway. He was wearing jeans and a long-sleeved dark gray Henley that made his eyes the most beautiful man's eyes I'd ever seen. He leaned against the doorframe, not coming further into the room.

"Hey," he said.

"Hi," I said, momentarily stupid with surprise and lust and pure happiness to see him. It pulsed over me like someone had doused me with water. He was *here*.

"Jimmy texted me," Damon said when I did nothing but stare at him like an idiot. "He said you were drowning your sorrows and you might need a ride home." His gaze moved down to the glass in my hand, which I'd just filled with beer. "You're drowning your sorrows in stout?"

I looked down. I'd pulled the handle with the owl on it when I filled the glass, and now some kind of pitch-black liquid was in my beer glass. "I don't know," I said. "Apparently." I took a tiny sip and nearly gagged. "Dear God, what is this? Do we actually sell it?"

The corner of his mouth twitched, but he didn't smile. He also stayed in his spot in the doorway. My Doberman, who never assumed. "Stout is an acquired taste," he said.

"Acquired by people who are clinically insane." I dumped

the beer down the bar sink and rinsed the glass. "So much for that experiment."

"Any particular reason you're trying to get drunk?" Damon asked.

You, I thought. *I miss you and I don't know how to handle it.* "It's been a rough few weeks," I said lamely instead.

"You seem to be doing okay. I like the new name."

I brightened at that. I'd officially changed the name of the Wild Wild West to just the Wild. I'd had a new sign put up, one that didn't look like a holdover from the eighties. I was getting a new website and new marketing materials made—thank you, bank loan—and there was a banner beneath the new sign that said *Under New Management.* "Do you honestly like it?" I asked Damon. "Please tell me the truth."

"Yes, I like it," he replied softly. "You've done a great job. And I always tell you the truth."

Oh, that hit me in the gut. I bit my lip. "About that. We need to talk."

Damon reached one of his gorgeous, masculine hands up—I missed those hands—and scratched his temple uncomfortably. "No, I don't really think we do."

"We do. About that night—"

"There's nothing to say."

"There's plenty to say. I'm really sorry—"

"I don't need to hear it, Andie. You don't owe me anything."

He was shutting me out. It was probably a reflex, just like it had been when I did it. Except with Damon, it was born of so many years being lonely.

Even though I'd been married, I'd been lonely, too. And I was suddenly tired of it. So tired I didn't want to be that way for one more day.

"I owe you everything," I told him. "You changed my life."

"*You* changed your life."

Were we going to argue about this? "Fine, I changed it. But I leaned on you, and that felt good." Now I sounded like I needed him as a prop. So I swallowed and womaned up. "I miss you."

Damon rubbed a hand over his face, and for the first time I noticed a trace of exhaustion in the line of his body, the way he leaned on the doorframe. I'd been blinded by how good he looked. But Jimmy had said he was miserable. Because of me.

"You miss me, too," I said. "Jimmy told me you do. You like me."

"I'm no good at this," he said.

That made me laugh. "Neither am I." I rounded the bar and approached him slowly. I didn't want him to back out that door and out of my life again.

Damon didn't flee, so I came even closer. I couldn't go another minute without touching him, so I took one of his hands in mine. It was warm and strong. How had I missed his hands this much? How had I missed all of him this much?

I curled his hand around mine, watched how it dwarfed mine. He gripped me lightly. He didn't pull me closer, but he didn't back away.

I dropped a kiss to the warm skin on the back of his hand. "I'm very sorry," I whispered. "Can you forgive me?"

His hand flexed in mine, and he pulled free. For a second I panicked, and then his hands were cradling my face, warm and strong and familiar. When I breathed, I breathed him in.

"I just want to take care of you," he said, his voice low and ragged. "I did all of it for you, and I didn't mean to hurt you. I would never hurt you. *Never.* Do you understand that?"

I nodded. Tears spilled from my eyes and down my cheeks. "I shouldn't have doubted you."

"I'm not mad about that," Damon said. "I'm not mad about

anything. I just want you to be safe and to have the life you deserve. Even if it doesn't include me."

I sniffed. "It has to include you. I'm not happy if my life doesn't have you in it."

He made a sound of pain and leaned in. I felt the touch of his scruff on my skin, and he placed a lingering kiss to my neck, as if he couldn't help himself. I grabbed him, twisting my hands into his shirt. I was not going to let him go. Not now, not ever.

"What do you want?" he asked me.

"I want to go back to that day at the house, when we were in bed," I said. "When I asked you to be my boyfriend and you said yes. I want there to be an us. I want you to meet my son and be part of his life. I want you to be mine every day, and I want to be yours. *That's* what I want."

"Andie." His voice was rough. "I'm not a good bet."

"You're the best bet," I told him. "I should know. Do you know what I see when I look at you?" I didn't let him answer. "I see a man who fights his demons every day. Just gets up and fights, over and over again, no matter how many times he has to. You're the bravest person I've ever known."

He was quiet for a moment. I listened to him breathing.

"I don't deserve you," he said at last. "You think I don't know it? I fucking know it. And yet I'm not leaving."

"Good," I said, because despite the moment, those words made me giddy. Damon was here, and he wasn't leaving. I tilted my face up to his as I leaned in, pressing my body against his.

He was warm against me, and I felt my body thrum when it touched his. He dropped his hands and I parted my lips to say something, perhaps to protest or to keep trying to convince him, but I didn't get the chance to speak. Damon kissed me.

I leaned into it, kissing him back. Around us, the bar was dim and quiet. There was no one here but me, kissing Damon, claiming him as mine. For good this time.

He broke the kiss, raising his hands to my face again as if it was precious. "This is not going to be easy, Andie," he said. "We both have rough edges. But I'm in."

"So am I." I put my hands on his waist, curling them into the warm fabric of his shirt again. "Take me home?"

He smiled a little, that smile that made my knees weak. "You sure? We're alone here. I've never had sex on a bar, have you?"

I smiled back at him as my blood warmed. "You put a camera behind the bar, you pervert."

"I can turn it off. I set up the security system, remember?"

I rose up and brushed my lips along his jawline, feeling his body get tight beneath my hands.

"Just kiss me, please," I said, "and take me home. I'm finally going to cook you dinner."

EPILOGUE

Damon

One year later

The sun was starting to set when I pulled into the driveway. It was a beautiful spring evening in Colorado. When I got out of the car, I noticed that the front lawn needed mowing.

Yes, that was me, Damon Blake. Thinking about my fucking lawn.

Life had taken me to some strange places. And now I was here.

Not only did I have a lawn, I had a house—actually, Andie and I had a house. She'd sold the old one she'd lived in with Terry and we'd bought one that was all our own. It wasn't huge, it wasn't fancy, but it was ours.

I hefted my bag onto my shoulder, picked up my shopping bags, and walked over the lengthening grass. There was a chair with a little table next to it on the front porch—Andie's. There was a pile of fragrant sneakers just inside the front door—those belonged to Miles and his friends.

In the front room, which was the living room, I glanced at the framed photo on the wall above the sofa. It was a large print of the jumbled houses of Positano, Italy, built on the sheer cliff face rising up from the sea. It was taken by Kat, my sister-in-law, on her wedding trip with Alex. Kat was a famous photographer now, and the print was probably worth money, though we would never sell it. It had been a housewarming gift when we bought our place. Alex and Kat had delivered it in person when they visited the month after we moved in. Andie, Miles, and I reciprocated with a visit to Texas during Miles's spring break. I was the guy who made him mow the lawn, but Miles thought his Uncle Alex was very cool.

As for the rest of us adults? We not only got along, we had started to relax together and have fun. My brother was my brother again—more so, maybe, than he'd ever been. The past was finally the past.

The front room was empty and quiet. I knew Andie was home because her car was here, and Miles was here with his friends, but they were nowhere in sight. I dropped my bag, took off my own shoes, and walked into the kitchen with the shopping bags. As I put a couple cans of soda in the fridge, I listened carefully.

There were voices in the basement. So Miles and his friends were playing video games, then. There was a shout as someone probably got killed in the game, and then laughter. Then ribbing. Ah, to be fourteen again.

Or maybe not.

I took one of the grocery bags and opened the basement door. "Miles," I called down.

In a second he appeared at the bottom of the stairs, smiling up at me. He had grown taller in the past year, started to fill out in the shoulders. He was a handsome kid, and thank God, he looked nothing like Terry. Those cheekbones were all Andie's, though his hair was lighter, and he had it cut in the same style his friends all had. Someday he would be very embarrassed about that haircut. I didn't tease him about it, but I took lots of pictures so I could torture him with them in ten years.

"Hey, man," Miles said. "What's up?"

We weren't father and son, Miles and me, but to my surprise, we had gotten close really fast. Maybe it was the formative experience of me helping him puke when we first met. Maybe it was just our personalities. But as I slid into Andie's life, I had also slid into Miles's, and to both of our surprise, it had felt really good.

"You're on lawn duty," I told him.

He frowned. "Not now?"

"No, not now. Tomorrow morning."

He grinned. "What do I get for it?"

I felt myself smiling back. "The pleasure of being useful."

"And fifty bucks?"

"Fifty? Dream on, kid."

"I'm willing to go as low as forty."

He was already saving for his first car, so this was a delicate negotiation. "You get twenty-five if it's done before noon. If it's done after, you only get ten."

"Ten bucks?" Miles pretended to be offended. "I can barely buy anything for ten bucks. You want me to starve?"

"You're not going to starve." I held up the grocery bag. "Catch."

His face lit up. "Sweet!"

I reached into the grocery bag, took out a bag of chips, and tossed it down the stairs at him. He caught it and, in turn, tossed it to his friends. I heard a cheer go up from somewhere in the basement, probably the sofa in front of the TV.

I pulled out another bag of chips, and another. Apparently you feed a teenage boy by throwing chips at him and his friends. When I was finished, Miles thanked me and went back to his video game. I closed the basement door.

That took care of him for a while. Now for Andie.

She was probably upstairs. We had turned the extra bedroom into a small office. Sometimes Andie used it, and sometimes I did. I didn't have a permanent office because I was on the road a lot during the day. Andie still had her office at the Wild, but the home office was handy when she wanted to do some work from home in off hours.

I opened the door to the office, and sure enough, there she was. Andie was sitting behind the desk in old yoga pants and a stretched-out tee, her dark curls tied up on top of her head. She had no makeup on. She had a pen in her hand and she was peering at something on the screen.

When she saw me, her lips parted in shock. The pen fell to the surface of the desk with a click.

"Holy hell, you're wearing a suit," she said.

"I know. I told you, I had to go to court today."

Her eyes traveled up and down me, over and over. "Uh," she said, lost for words for a second. I hadn't been wearing the suit when I left this morning; I'd changed in the bathroom at the courthouse. That was how much I hated wearing a fucking suit.

"Earth to Andie," I said.

"Uh huh." She cleared her throat. "How was court?"

"It was court. They asked me questions, I answered. I left."

I had gotten certified and started my own business as a private investigator. I liked it. Along with the fact that it was surprisingly lucrative, I was my own boss, I was rarely in an

office, and I spent my days however the hell I wanted. Except
for the days when a case I had worked on landed in court and I
needed to testify. It was rare, but it happened from time to
time.

Andie was still running the Wild, which was doing killer
business. She was bringing in the younger crowd—not just the
college kids but the people in their twenties and thirties. She
was using the stage in the huge space to book really good live
bands, and sometimes DJ's so the crowd would get dancing.
The Wild had gone from an old fashioned joke to a hotspot,
and it was all because of Andie. She'd even hired a manager to
help with the day-to-day operations so she didn't have to do the
hours she used to.

My girl, it turned out, was a brilliant businesswoman.

Maybe she liked how I looked in the suit, but I liked how
she looked in the old yoga pants and tee. I liked Andie in
anything. And in nothing. "What are you doing?" I asked her.

She licked her lip. "Something with numbers. I don't really
remember."

"Okay then, stop what you're doing and come with me."

She was out of her chair and rounding her desk in an
instant. "Where are we going?"

I gave her a meaningful look. "You said you liked the suit."

"We can't." She lowered her voice to a whisper, a mother's
reflex. "You know Miles is home."

"He's in the basement playing video games with his friends.
I threw chips at them. We have an hour at least." The boys,
eternally hungry, would emerge, probably seeking pizza. But
not yet.

Her eyes widened, and I knew I had her. There was
nothing that turned Andie on more than a forbidden thrill.
"We'll have to be fast," she whispered. "And we have to lock the
door."

Our bedroom door had a lock on it, of course. You think I was going to go without one?

I took her hand and turned it so the palm was up. I kissed her wrist, feeling her quickening pulse beneath my lips.

She moaned a little. "Oh, my God. That suit."

"You're wasting time, Andie."

She literally jumped me. She put her arms around my neck and wrapped her legs tightly around my waist as I caught her, gripping her ass through the old yoga pants. It was a good thing I kept myself in shape. Before I could carry her down the hall, she pulled me down and kissed me, long and deep.

"Have I told you that you make me happy today?" she asked against my mouth.

"No," I said as I maneuvered her toward our bedroom.

"Well, you do." She kissed my neck as I banged the door open.

"You make me happy, too," I said, and I meant it. The only thing I wanted was to make this woman happy. Forever.

We'd start right now.

And I'd start by taking off the suit.

Made in the USA
Columbia, SC
20 December 2021

52391117R00121